THEY ALL HAD A ~~FEAR~~

MICHELE LEATHERS

To my parents.
Your strength, love, and unwavering support
have shaped so much of who I am and hope to become.

Copyright © 2021, 2026 by Michele Leathers
Cover and internal design © 2026 by Sourcebooks
Cover design by Casey Moses
Cover image © Natalia Ganelin/Arcangel, Vector-World/Shutterstock, bdvect 1/Shutterstock

Sourcebooks and the colophon are registered trademarks of Sourcebooks.

All rights reserved. No part of this book may be reproduced in any form or by any electronic or mechanical means, including information storage and retrieval systems—except in the case of brief quotations embodied in critical articles or reviews—without permission in writing from its publisher, Sourcebooks.

No part of this book may be used or reproduced in any manner for the purpose of training artificial intelligence technologies or systems.

The characters and events portrayed in this book are fictitious or are used fictitiously. Any similarity to real persons, living or dead, is purely coincidental and not intended by the author.

Published by Sourcebooks Fire, an imprint of Sourcebooks
1935 Brookdale RD, Naperville, IL 60563-2773
(630) 961-3900
sourcebooks.com

Originally self-published as *They All Had a Fear* in 2021 by Michele Leathers.

Cataloging-in-Publication Data is on file with the Library of Congress.

The authorized representative in the EEA is Dorling Kindersley Verlag GmbH. Arnulfstr. 124, 80636 Munich, Germany

Manufactured in the UK by Clays and distributed by
Dorling Kindersley Limited, London
001-358267-Mar/26
10 9 8 7 6 5 4 3 2 1

CHAPTER 1

WINTER

Deaths always come in threes. People might call that an old saying or a superstition, but I believed it was true. Back in Utah, when my friend Venus Swensen was murdered by her ex-boyfriend, he also killed her younger brother and sister. Three dead. Here in North Carolina, there had already been two deaths, of my Aunt Emma and her fiancé Reginald, which meant a third was coming, and soon.

Through the bug-splattered windshield, my eyes traveled up the large staircase that led to the front door of Aunt Emma's house. This place was nothing like the boxy, stilted beach houses down the road or across the street. From where I sat, I couldn't even see the rooftop, it was so tall. Despite the fact that it was a hundred degrees outside today and probably a hundred and twenty inside the SUV, I felt a cold shiver snake down my spine as I thought about what had happened inside this house.

Mom grabbed my arm, smiling at me. "Winter, just look at how beautiful this place is. It's a mansion!" She squealed like a game show contestant who had just won a big prize.

I wished she would stop. I pulled away, refusing to celebrate with her in spite of what I was seeing.

Mom and I had inherited this house from Aunt Emma, and that was a huge game changer for us. The nicest place we had ever lived before was a single-wide trailer with a hole in the living room floor that we covered up with a piece of plywood and a rug. (Yes, people tripped over it all the time.) Mom would likely spend the rest of her life here. Odds were, I would too. There was no going back to Utah. All I knew for certain was that in the fall I would be starting my senior year of high school here—an unfamiliar place with no friends.

"Beach life, here we come!" Mom cheered, tucking a strand of sandy blond hair behind her ear. The bright sun reflected off her silver hoop earring. She did her happy dance, bouncing around in her seat like she was a teenager, a forty-year-old teenager.

But I couldn't share her enthusiasm. I couldn't even crack a smile. "Yeah. Here's to beach life," I muttered. "Sun, surf, and suppressed emotions."

Mom shouldn't have been so happy. We had just picked up Aunt Emma's ashes from the funeral home. That was our first stop when we arrived in Kure Beach. What bothered me the most about Mom's behavior was that I felt like she was genuinely glad her sister had died. To say that Mom hated

Aunt Emma wasn't a strong enough statement to describe how she really felt about her. The last time they spoke to each other was eight years ago, when I was ten.

The SUV's door squealed as I pushed it open and climbed out. The smell of the salty sea air quickly replaced the odor of greasy fast-food wrappers and stale french fries. Mom started taking pictures of the house with her phone. I turned to look at the cardboard box sitting in the back seat that held Aunt Emma's ashes. *I'm sorry*, I thought to myself, wishing that she was still alive so she could hear me.

I wanted to hold a funeral service for Aunt Emma, but Mom was opposed to this idea. She argued that there weren't any other family members besides us to invite. Still, I thought we should do something, maybe have a minister perform a eulogy, and Mom and I would dress up in black. But pretending like Aunt Emma never existed and ignoring the fact that she died only made me feel worse.

When we were at the funeral home, I begged Mom—once again—to hold a funeral service for Aunt Emma. Mom glared at me and said, "I highly doubt that your aunt had any friends to invite."

Like Mom had room to talk. She went through friends like tissues. But sadly, she was probably right. Aunt Emma tended to center her entire life around one person, and that one person was usually whoever she was dating or engaged to at the time. This last guy she was engaged to, Reginald Fontaine, must have expected that she would actually follow through and marry him, because he left her everything in his will. And when Aunt Emma died, she left everything to me and Mom. I had hoped Mom might feel at least a little gratitude and want to pay her respects, but even in death she couldn't find any respect for her sister.

I had never met Reginald, so I didn't know anything about him. Aunt Emma's estate attorney, Mr. Davis, told us that he passed away from a heart attack on April first. Yes, on April Fools' Day. Then Aunt Emma died on April thirteenth. Friday the thirteenth. Bad luck and irony. I wondered what might come next.

Mom started walking toward the house. Hopefully there wasn't a black cat about to cross our path.

"Wait," I said, pointing back to the SUV. "Don't forget the ashes."

"It'll be fine. We can get that later."

No, it won't be fine, and you know it. "We can't leave Aunt Emma in here."

"Why not? It's not like it's gonna kill her. She's already dead."

"Mom!" I glared at her, horrified. I couldn't believe she said that out loud.

"You're always such a worrier, Winter. Trust me. It's fine." She waved me off like I was being ridiculous. As if abandoning a dead relative in the back seat was normal behavior.

I picked up the box that contained Aunt Emma's ashes, then caught up to Mom, walking past tall palm trees and flowering bushes. At the edge of the manicured front lawn

I could see a path made of crushed shells and sand disappear around the corner of the house. The roar of ocean waves crashed in the distance. I guessed the path must lead to the beach. I continued up the front steps.

The sprawling porch and huge double doors made me feel like I was stepping into a fairy tale. In spite of this being an older home, it appeared to be in pristine condition. The deep purple paint might have felt loud or tacky anywhere else, but here, against its crisp white trim it looked elegant. I felt the tension in my neck and shoulders start to relax. Something about the color purple has always had a calming effect on me. I loved it so much that I dyed the ends of my blond hair purple, giving an ombre effect.

Mom reached inside her overflowing purse, fishing around for the house key. Unable to find it, she set her purse down on the welcome mat and began emptying everything out. "I can't wait to see what it looks like inside," she said as she peered up at me, grinning. "Winter, you're going to love it here—I just know you will. We were made for beach life."

As if saying the same thing over and over makes it true—but she couldn't have been more wrong. Maybe she was made for beach life, with her sun-kissed hair and perfect tan, but I wasn't. Not at all. Whenever I spent time in the sun, my skin started at white, then went straight to red, immediately followed by regret. I had been named *Winter*, the exact opposite of summer. Plus, I couldn't even swim. I did not belong here.

I leaned against the porch railing and turned my attention to the coral-colored house next door. With expansive balconies on its second and third floors, it was just as beautiful and grand as Aunt Emma's. A dune buggy with big bumpy wheels sat tucked inside the garage. I had to admit, that vehicle actually looked like a lot of fun. I wondered if Aunt Emma had one of those parked inside her garage too.

As my eyes continued to scan the house next door, I noticed a person's silhouette hovering in the upstairs window behind a sheer curtain. The dark shadow remained motionless, even though I was staring directly at it.

I turned my attention to Mom again. She was still searching for the house key.

Instead of taking in the rest of the view around me, my eyes focused on a single palm tree, not because I was admiring it. I was trying to act like nothing was wrong. But in truth, I was becoming increasingly anxious. I swear I could still feel that person in the window staring at us, just like I could feel the heat from the sun.

After several long seconds, maybe a minute, I turned and looked up at the window again. My stomach dipped. The shadow was still there. I immediately dropped my gaze as if I hadn't noticed, as if I wasn't extremely bothered by the fact that Mom and I were under surveillance by some stranger.

A normal person wouldn't stand there and stare like that, not unless they were trying to send a message like *I'm a pervert and I'm watching you*, or *I'm nosy and I'm judging you*, or *I'm a murderer and I'm going to kill you.* I didn't believe I was being paranoid to think these things. I was only being realistic.

"Here we go!" Mom pulled out two house keys and slid one of them into the lock.

Before walking inside, I looked up at the window one last time—just as a hand appeared, parting the curtains. A cold sensation settled upon me like a storm cloud. Goose bumps raced down my arms. I could make out the outline of a person's shoulders, their neck, and a baseball cap on top of their head, but couldn't see a face. Whoever was staring at me wasn't just being a nosy neighbor. I could feel that this person was much worse—way more sinister. Darkness radiated from them. I could feel it all the way to my bones. No longer able to contain my fear, I turned and rushed inside the house, slamming the door behind me.

I stood there, my entire body tense, heart pounding rapidly, my hands clutching the box of Aunt Emma's ashes. Slowly the room started coming into focus. I felt as though I had been transported to another world and became fully engrossed in my surroundings. This was not what I expected. From the outside, this house looked like a vacation postcard with a brightly colored beach vibe, but inside there was no hint of the beach anywhere, not a single seashell, mermaid, or picture of the ocean.

Everywhere I looked something glistened and sparkled, catching the light from the sun shining through the windows. Crystal chandeliers hung from the ceiling. Glass sconces and mirrors adorned the walls. White marble tiles sprawled across the floors. The glass tables had even more glass on top of them: etched bowls, decorative lamps, and vases. I was almost afraid to touch anything for fear that I might break it. Even the tiniest piece of broken glass could penetrate the skin and draw blood.

Mom looked around the living room, eyes wide, smile even wider. "Doesn't this place just take your breath away?" She spun around, her skirt flaring out like a flower in full bloom. "I feel like a princess in an ice castle."

Doesn't ice melt in the sun? I wanted to ask but I didn't.

Mom disappeared somewhere as I began exploring the rest of the first floor on my own. I discovered that each room was similar in style, with only a slight change in color: the living room was white, the dining room was off-white, the family room was beige, the kitchen was buttercream yellow, and the bathroom was ivory.

I set Aunt Emma's ashes down on the bookshelf in the living room right next to an intricately carved crystal vase. Out of all the shiny pieces in the room, this one caught my eye the most, probably because it had such a complex pattern etched into it and looked the most expensive.

I wondered if the rest of the house was decorated the same way. I sure hoped not.

The massive staircase leading upstairs was probably six feet wide from bottom to top. A crystal chandelier hung directly above it, resembling an upside-down wedding cake with lots of layers. My fingers trailed along the glass banister's smooth surface, then suddenly I remembered what Mr. Davis had told us. He said that Aunt Emma fell on these stairs. She was still conscious enough to call 911, but by the time the ambulance arrived, she had already died from her injuries.

"Winter!" Mom called with urgency in her voice.

A rush of adrenaline swept through me, and I took off running to find her.

Mom was standing in the family room, looking out the sliding glass door. "There's something going on out there," she said as she slid the door open, letting in a waft of hot, humid air.

I followed her out to the back deck, amazed at the view laid out before my eyes. Seagulls hovered in the clear blue sky above. Just beyond the back fence, people and umbrellas dotted the billowy sand. The massive ocean dominating the scenery, stretching out as far as I could see. Fierce waves crashed, one after another, the noise a constant roar in my ears.

As I gazed upon the beautiful landscape, I noticed something unexpected. Farther down the beach to my right, a crowd of people hovered behind a barrier consisting of orange caution cones and yellow police tape.

Mom started down the path toward the beach. "Let's go see what happened."

I almost followed her but thought better of it. There was something I needed to do first. "I'm going to go get my shoes.

I'll meet you out there." I turned around to go back inside so I could make sure the front door was locked.

With my flip-flops on and two house keys in hand, I locked the back door and headed to the beach, curious about what was going on. I found Mom all the way at the front of the crowd of onlookers. "Excuse me," I said, nudging past the people around her.

As I stood next to her, my eyes widened in surprise. I was finally able to see what she and everybody else was staring at. The shape under the white sheet made it perfectly clear.

There was a dead body.

CHAPTER 2

MILTON

I sometimes dreamed—or rather I had hoped—that I had been switched at birth, that someone had snatched me away from my real parents, parents who were nurturing and loving, parents who adored and wanted me. I daydreamed about these parents. I imagined what our house was like: a warm fire in the fireplace, a cozy couch to sit on, all the cereal I could ever eat stocked in the cupboards, a bedroom of my own. This fantasy helped me get through the tough times. And in my fantasy, I was also an only child.

When I was five, I went to the beach with my *so-called* parents. My alleged brother was there too. He asked if he could bury me in the sand, and I told him no several times, but he wouldn't stop pestering me; that's what he always did. He was relentless, and he always got his way.

My brother eventually complained to Mom, claiming that

I didn't want to play with him, and that I was being mean. Mom didn't want to be bothered. I doubted she ever wanted kids. We were a nuisance to her. For some reason, those natural mothering instincts never existed in her. She reminded me of a cold rock at the bottom of the river—smooth and pretty on the outside, but absolutely hard to the core and useless.

Mom huffed in irritation, listening to my brother complain, then she turned to me, rolling her eyes. "Just let your brother bury you. Stop being so difficult."

Dad pulled off his headphones, wondering what the problem was. Mom explained that I wasn't being nice to my brother, which wasn't true.

I knew right then that I had a choice to make: either face Dad's wrath or deal with my brother. I chose the lesser of two evils. My brother.

The hole we were digging was located behind our parents. My brother had picked this spot on purpose. He knew they wouldn't be able to see or hear us.

In the process of digging, I found a shark tooth mixed in with all the sand. My brother wanted it, but I refused to give it to him. I was the one who had found it—it belonged to me.

I kept the shark tooth clenched tightly in my hand as I sat inside the deep hole, while my brother started shoveling sand over the top of me.

My entire body was soon covered—even my face. I held my breath and shut my eyes, totally helpless, unable to move or break free from the pit. I thought I was going to die. I started panicking, unsure how much longer I could hold my breath. In my mind I was screaming, pleading for someone to rescue me. My parents didn't come to save me. An old lady did.

She knelt beside me, brushing the sand from my face as I sucked in fresh air. She had a thick stripe of white sunscreen across her nose and short purplish-gray hair.

"Are you okay?" she asked, patting my back while I coughed.

At first I couldn't speak. My throat felt raspy, full of gritty sand. It was even in my nose. I bent over, gagging, until I was finally able to clear my throat.

"Are you okay?" she asked again, squinting to get a better look at me.

I nodded and coughed some more. "I'm fine," I croaked, grateful to still be alive; grateful to this old lady for saving me.

"You sure?" she asked, studying my face.

"Yeah," I coughed. "I'm good." I really wasn't good. I wasn't fine either. I had almost been murdered by my own brother. Not once did *he* ask me if I was okay. There wasn't even a hint of remorse in his smug expression. He just stood there watching me gasping, a sly smile playing on his chapped lips.

"What kind of foolishness is this? Burying this little boy," the old lady said, wagging a finger at my brother. "Did you get tired of kicking over his sandcastle?"

My father pulled his headphones off and nudged Mom. Still on her towel, she craned her neck toward the old lady. "Excuse me. Can I help you with something?"

The old lady aimed her finger at Mom. "You should have been watching them."

"And you should mind your own business," Mom snapped.

The old lady fired right back. "You're lucky I don't call the authorities. This little boy almost suffocated."

Dad held up his hands. "Now hold on. Let's not get overexcited."

I kept coughing, still struggling to breathe. Neither of my parents even bothered to check on me. They were both too busy arguing with the old lady. They should have been thanking her.

Utterly frustrated, the old lady told Mom, "The next time you come to the beach, try packing a little common sense." She looked back at me and pointed to the shark tooth still clutched in my hand. "That's a big one," she said. "A rare find and lucky too." Then she gave my parents a final parting glare before marching off.

My brother was jealous that I found the shark tooth, and I figured that it must be something pretty special for him to want it so badly. I may not have been able to defend myself against him, but I had something he didn't. Keeping this shark tooth wasn't exactly a way for me to get revenge for what he had done to me. But it was the next best thing. Time would tell if it would be lucky or not.

CHAPTER 3

TAMARA (BELLANY)

I knew going to Burgaw was a risk. It was only an hour and a half from Smithfield—my hometown, the place where I met my boyfriend Quentin. The same place where my life went off the rails and I was forced to run. The cops there were still looking for me—or the girl I used to be, Bellany Silverfield. Now I went by Tamara. Even though I had changed my name and appearance, I knew there was a chance of bumping into someone from my past. I actually never intended on setting foot in North Carolina again. But since fortune brought me here, I decided to drive up to the cemetery in Burgaw where Quentin had been buried.

I went late, to avoid people. It took a little while to find his family plot in the dark. I wondered what I would feel when I saw his name etched into the headstone—sadness, loss, maybe even grief? I kicked off my shoes, grass under my feet, knowing that his body was buried underneath all that dirt. He was gone forever.

I wondered if any real tears would fall from my eyes. Crying was something I could do on demand. It was easy, and I frequently used it as a tool to manipulate people. But there was no one here to put on a show for.

I knew when I left the cemetery that I would never return. Quentin was a past boyfriend, a partner in crime, someone who I had relied on, but he had also royally messed things up for me.

Because of Quentin, I missed out on that hundred-thousand-dollar reward my father put up when he thought I had been murdered. All Quentin had to do was frame Charlotte like we had planned. But no. He let his emotions get in the way and almost got us both caught. We had to go on the run with nothing.

When I came up with my next score in Washington, Quentin ruined things again. I missed out on inheriting a hotel, an amazing house, and a big fat bank account. If he had just gotten rid of that girl, Samantha, like I told him, then everything would have worked out fine. But once again he failed to stick to the plan, only this time he got himself killed.

Surviving on the run without money was impossible. My life had become incredibly difficult, and Quentin was the reason.

I decided not to leave the flowers I had brought with me.

He didn't deserve them, not even in death. I threw the flowers in a trash can.

It turned out that I didn't miss Quentin after all. I wasn't even sad that he was gone.

CHAPTER 4

WINTER

A couple police officers walked by, stopping in front of me and blocking my view of the dead body. I figured there wasn't much to see anyway since it was covered up. My gaze traveled over to the ocean as the waves spilled out to shore, and I caught sight of something curious. There was a flat path left in the sand, connecting the water's edge to the spot where the body had been laid. Whatever happened to this person happened in the water and their body was dragged up to shore.

The officers finally moved, and I saw the body again, only this time something new caught my eye. Spilling out from the top of the sheet, mixed in with all of the sand, were several strands of long blond hair. A girl was under there.

I tried not to lean against or touch the yellow police tape that had been strung out to block off the area, but this was difficult since the people behind me kept creeping forward inch by inch. Mom didn't seem to mind being squished in with all the other concerned beachgoers.

She craned her neck to eavesdrop on a nearby conversation that I couldn't hear. I wondered if anyone knew what happened to that girl. I felt like it was important to find out, since Mom and I were going to be living here and beach life was something we were totally unfamiliar with. Did this kind of thing happen all the time? Just how dangerous was that ocean?

I leaned closer to Mom, in an effort to keep our conversation just between us. "Did they say how she died?" I asked.

"They don't know." Mom shrugged. "Maybe she drowned."

The muttering voices around us grew louder, then suddenly one rose above all the rest. It was a high-pitched voice that kept saying, "Excuse me. Excuse me." Then I saw who the voice belonged to. A blond girl wearing a seriously skimpy bikini. She had managed to work her way to the front of the crowd, right next to me. She reached up and swept her hair off her face. "Do you know what happened?" she asked me.

"No, I just got here."

"I'm Tamara Gold, by the way."

Mom reached across me. "My name's Sasha Covington, and this is my daughter, Winter."

Mom and Tamara continued to speculate about what might have happened to the girl. I really wasn't listening.

Tamara's nose looked slightly swollen and red around

the nostrils. I had never seen a person with a fresh nose job before, but if I were to guess what the healing process looked like, I would have to say it looked like that. I wondered if she used to have a huge beak of a nose or something truly odd-looking. My best guess was that her nose probably just wasn't perfect enough for her standards. She also looked like she had breast implants. It kind of bothered me that she had multiple plastic surgeries done at such a young age. She didn't look much older than me. I had heard about people who were addicted to plastic surgery. What was she planning on changing next?

Both Mom and Tamara were taller than me and were talking over me. Literally. I took a step back, letting them continue without me being caught in the crossfire. A man next to me bumped against my arm with his sweaty skin. I recoiled in disgust. "Mom, I'm gonna get out of here." I handed her one of the house keys.

"Okay, honey. I'll meet you back at the house." She didn't look at me when she said that. Her eyes were glued to the scene in front of her.

I quickly weaved through the crowd, trying not to touch anyone. As I approached the lifeguard tower, I saw two male lifeguards stationed there.

The tower wasn't that high up off the ground, maybe eight feet. It was just a basic platform with a ladder leading up to it. The two guys standing at the top were leaning against the railing, mostly looking out toward the ocean, but occasionally they would cast a glance toward the crowd of people surrounding the dead girl.

One of the lifeguards was blond, the other had dark curly hair. The blond one had a noticeably flabby stomach, a true muffin top. He was chewing gum and blowing bright green bubbles. He was the one who talked the most, yet he still somehow managed to blow several bubbles. I figured he was the type of person who only had two volumes: loud and louder. In general, loud talkers irritated me, especially when they stood too close. Those two things usually went hand in hand—close and loud. Not a good combination.

I slowed my walk to listen in when I realized they were talking about the dead girl.

"There was nothing we could have done to save her, Eli," the blond, loud talker said. "She was already dead." After a few more chomps on his gum, he blew another large green bubble, almost the size of his head.

The other lifeguard, Eli, stared blankly at the crowd of onlookers, his dark hair in tight, wet ringlets. "That doesn't make me feel any better," he replied.

Their conversation was definitely something I wanted to continue listening to. I chose a spot close by, sat down, and started sifting through the sand like my sole purpose for being there was to look for shells.

The blond lifeguard popped another bubble, leaned back, and propped his foot up on the railing. "Was that your first time ever seeing a dead body?" he asked.

"What kind of a question is that, Jaxson?" Eli replied, thick irritation in his voice.

"Calm down, dude," Jaxson snapped. "I was just trying to make conversation." He blew another bubble then spit his gum out over the railing.

"I don't want to step on another piece of your disgusting gum. Go pick it up."

"Fine!" Jaxson climbed down the ladder, then glanced up to see if Eli was watching him—which he wasn't—so he kicked some sand over the top of his gum and left it there. I could have predicted he would do that. Then Jaxson cleared his throat, spit on the ground, and climbed back up the ladder.

Jaxson truly seemed annoying. I had sympathy for Eli since he had to put up with him all day long. But I wasn't interested in listening to them bicker. I wanted them to say something else about the dead girl. I wanted to know what happened to her.

Several minutes of silence passed, and I was about to leave when Jaxson started talking about their high school robotics club. Well, that's random, I thought. What happened to the dead girl conversation? Jaxson laughed, talking about the robot they had built. Apparently, someone had stolen it.

I gotta say, I did not peg these two as being members of a robotics club. They seemed like the type to be on the swim team, or the wrestling team, maybe even the football team, but the robotics club? Seriously?

Since their conversation was no longer of interest to me, I

stood up and started brushing the sand off my legs. I dropped a couple shells into my pocket, nothing really that special, but this was my first time at the beach, and I had never collected shells before.

I looked up at the lifeguard tower again, and that's when I realized how close it was to my house. In fact, it was exactly in front of it.

Jaxson had pulled out a mirror and was looking at his reflection while spiking up his hair with some gel. There was something about a guy who cared too much about his appearance that just grated on my nerves. I already wasn't impressed with him. That whole spitting out his gum and covering it with sand situation told me all I needed to know. He was a jerk.

Eli was watching the swimmers in the ocean, actually doing his job. From where I stood, I had a perfect view of his broad shoulders, the sharp taper in his waist, and the curls in his dark hair. I bet he had tons of girls fawning all over him. I probably shouldn't even waste my time, I thought to myself.

The only boyfriend I had ever had was Braden Bower when I was in the fourth grade. He was my first kiss. It was horrible. Our teeth bumped against each other. We never tried it again.

For me, in general, trying to meet a guy and get close to him was just something I wasn't good at. My friends had told me that I was too serious and needed to lighten up, laugh once in a while. Only the girls that flirted seemed to have boyfriends. Why couldn't a boy ever just be confident enough to flirt with me? It seemed like they all wanted to be chased. Well, I didn't want to chase anybody. I refused to do it.

Before I walked away, I turned my attention to the crowd surrounding the dead girl. I couldn't see Mom, but I figured she was there somewhere, probably talking to that Tamara chick. I bet she's the type of girl who eats her pizza with a fork and a knife so she won't get her fingers dirty.

What am I doing, I groaned to myself. I needed to stop this. Mom had told me that I was too critical and judgmental. But it was hard for me *not* to be this way. I truly had to work on stopping myself from venturing into the judgment zone. It was like my default mode, though. How does a person reset a default mode? I had no idea.

Okay, focus, I told myself. Forget about Tamara and concentrate on the dead girl again.

How did she die? If this was just a drowning incident, then why was all that yellow police tape strung out, and why were so many first responders there? It didn't make sense. There had to have been something else going on.

Eli and Jaxson probably knew the answers I was seeking, but I wasn't going to ask them. I didn't want to interrupt them while they were on the job. Besides, they would probably think I was just trying to flirt, and I did not want to be perceived as some kind of stupid, desperate-for-attention girl.

There had to have been someone else out here who knew what happened. I scanned my surroundings, searching for such a person. Three houses down from where I stood, there appeared to be some kind of a main road access. Several first responder vehicles were parked there. Perfect.

When I arrived at the edge of the parking lot, I kicked my flip-flops off, brushed the sand off my feet, then started searching for someone I could talk to.

An ambulance was parked nearby, and the back doors were open. There was a guy sitting inside wearing an EMT uniform. He stopped rummaging through a duffel bag when he saw me approach. He hopped out of the ambulance, then stood upright, towering over me. I am only five feet tall. He was at least six feet. The shiny gold name tag pinned to his shirt read NEVIN. He looked to be around my age, eighteen, or maybe a little older. He had a baby face, not a trace of a whisker on that tan skin of his. "Can I help you?" he asked.

I pointed behind me. "I was wondering if you could tell me what happened to that girl who died. Did she drown?"

He hesitated, trying to decide whether he should tell me. Then he made a face like he was about to say something unpleasant. I was prepared to hear whatever he had to say. My ears had probably already heard much worse. When your good friend and her little brother and sister get brutally murdered, there isn't much that can top that.

He let out a heavy sigh. "I'm not supposed to say anything, because this isn't official yet." He paused, glancing around to make sure no one could hear. "Her injuries were consistent with a shark attack."

"A shark attack?" I echoed in disbelief. Was he being serious?

"I really shouldn't be talking to anybody about this," he said in a hushed voice. "You're not a reporter, are you?"

He knew I wasn't a reporter. I was wearing a T-shirt, shorts, and flip-flops, not exactly professional attire. I shook my head, kind of irritated at his obvious attempt to flatter me. "Hardly," I replied.

"Well, you're definitely pretty enough to be one. I'd tune in and watch, that's for sure."

Hold up. Did this guy just drop a pickup line on *me*? Yes, he did. That almost never happened. Still, it hit me wrong. It wasn't what he said that bothered me. It was just that against the backdrop of a dead body, it creeped me out a little. If this was typical of how he approached girls, then I bet he got rejected all the time. In spite of his oversized self-confidence, I was not attracted to him in the slightest. If he was the magnet, I would be plastic.

"Nevin!" someone called.

Nevin cursed under his breath and slammed the doors of the ambulance shut. "I gotta go." He took off running toward the beach, catching up to another guy wearing a matching EMT uniform.

On my walk back to the house, my mind was flooded with questions. I wondered how old the dead girl was and if she was from around here. How far out was she swimming when she got attacked? Did Eli and Jaxson swim out to save her while the shark was still attacking her and put their own lives in danger?

I wondered if attacks like this one were usually fatal or if people sometimes survived. Since I wasn't really familiar with sharks or beach life, I wasn't sure. What surprised me most was how clean that sheet covering her was. Every inch of it was white. Shouldn't there have been more blood?

Why did Nevin think she was a shark attack victim? What kind of injuries did she have? Were there teeth marks? Was she missing a limb? I figured I would have to wait for the local news to explain what happened in order to find out the truth.

As I walked past the second house down from mine, I slowed my pace to see what kind of repairs the construction crew was doing. Definitely a new roof. They were scraping all the old shingles off. Workers were filtering in and out of the house through the back door. A man in his mid-forties stood only a few yards away from me. He was busily cutting wood and installing a new fence in the backyard. Eighties rock music blared from a boom box, occasionally being interrupted by the buzz of his saw. I stared at his severely outdated haircut. He actually had a mullet, and I think his hair was permed. A gold chain hung around his neck, and on his right shoulder there was a large tattoo of a shark with a girl in its mouth, blood squirting out.

Apparently I had been staring for too long, because he noticed. Our eyes met, and I don't know why I said this, but it just came flying out of my mouth. "I like this song." I said this really loud so he could hear me, only I wasn't sure if he did. He gave me a questioning look, and then carried on with his work.

I started toward home again. The music eventually faded away, but the song was still in my head: "Summer of '69," by Bryan Adams. Mom was a fan of eighties rock, so I knew most of her favorite songs and the lyrics.

My summer had just begun, yet the number of bad things that had happened were already starting to pile up. Aunt Emma had died, a scary person was living next door, and there was a dead girl on the beach. Would this be the best summer of my life, like the words to the song implied? No. Probably not. I certainly wasn't holding out much hope.

CHAPTER 5

MILTON

A couple days after I narrowly survived being buried alive, I caught my brother searching through my things in my bedroom.

"What are you doing?" I asked, already knowing that confronting him was gonna mean trouble for me.

My brother didn't bother to turn around. He kept rummaging through my things. "I was just looking for my charger. Relax."

"Don't tell me to relax," I snapped, racing across the room to get a closer look at what he was really doing. I knew he wasn't in here to look for his charger. That was a lie. "This is my room. Get out of here."

He spun around and cocked his fist back, making me flinch. "Back off," he warned, fist poised a few inches from my face.

"I-I'm gonna tell Mom," I said, unsure what else I could threaten him with. But even that wasn't really a threat.

"Go ahead," he said, pulling open another drawer. Instead of rummaging through it, he yanked it totally out and dumped it. My clothes scattered everywhere.

"Stop it!" I pleaded, helpless as he proceeded to dump every single one of my drawers out. "Mom!"

He cocked his fist back again, only this time I didn't flinch. I had already fallen for that once before. Then he lunged forward, right at me, and I cowered down, hands protecting my face.

He laughed at me, then gave me a swift kick in the stomach before slamming the door behind him.

I laid on the floor, writhing in pain, wishing I could call on Mom for help. But I knew she wouldn't be any help. She would probably get mad at me for interrupting her.

Then I reached down into my sock where I had my lucky shark tooth. I knew my brother had come in here to search for it. There wasn't anything else in here that he wanted. Ever since I found it, he had been trying to steal it from me.

I had been keeping it with me, either inside my pocket or tucked inside my sock, which wasn't all that comfortable. But that didn't matter. All I cared about was that I had it, he didn't, and even though I had no idea why he wanted it so badly, I was never going to let him have it.

A couple years later, when I turned ten, my school went on a field trip to the aquarium. I saw a variety of sharks that day, which absolutely amazed and thrilled me. I watched them swim around in the tank for as long as my teacher would let me. Then I headed to the display of the shark jawbones and teeth. I had never seen anything like it before. One of the jawbones was bigger than my entire body.

When my class was lining up to leave, I noticed that there was a gift shop, so I ran over to check it out. I found a plastic toy shark about four inches long. I waited until no one was looking, then I stuffed it in my pocket.

Later that day, my brother saw me playing with it and wanted to know where I had gotten it from. I lied and told him that I found it. He didn't believe me, but he also didn't tell on me. He just socked me in the shoulder really hard, giving me a bruise.

Then one day, my toy shark went missing. I searched through all of my brother's things but couldn't find it. He said that he had buried it in the backyard, and he wouldn't tell me where. It took me two solid months of digging to finally find it.

I had a lot of time to think while I was doing all that digging. I didn't just want my toy back. I wanted to defeat my enemy. I wanted my brother to know that he could never beat me. Somehow, in some way, I needed to change who I was. I needed to be transformed into something more. But how?

As time went on, I found myself drawn to the unexpected answer. It had been there all along, right in front of me. The ocean began calling to me, and I answered it.

It was the smell in the air, and the feel of the sand under my feet. It was the mysteriousness of the ocean that drew me in, and yet it was none of these things precisely. Out there, hidden in the depths of the endless sea, existed a whole other world—an entire ecosystem. Most people never see beyond the waves and tides. Their understanding of the sea and its beauty ends at the surface, but a perfect, inescapable yet harmonious struggle between life and death perpetually plays out in the depths below. This is what drew me to the ocean.

And what dominates this ecosystem? What holds the balance of aquatic nature and creation in its place? At the top of the pyramid is an apex predator so perfectly adapted to its role that it has ruled the seas for millennia. It is the shark.

I admired their strength, their status, their significance. No experienced swimmer dared provoke a shark. Only a fool would risk getting bit or maybe even killed, depending on the type of shark, by arousing its predatory instinct.

I wanted to be like them. I wanted people to think of me with the same kind of respect and fear they unquestioningly gave when a shark was near. I particularly wanted this from my family, but my brother and my parents refused to give me any respect. They treated me like I was at the bottom of the food chain. To them, I may as well have been algae slime.

My parents allowed my brother to terrorize and abuse me. He learned it from my father. My mother abused me too, mostly with her words. My parents could dish it out to my brother as well, but he was higher than me in the food chain. I was at the very bottom and everyone knew it.

I made a vow that one day, I would make them respect me. I would make them fear me. I would become the apex predator—the shark.

CHAPTER 6

WINTER

When I stepped inside the house, I was once again stunned by the fragile decor. This was going to take some getting used to.

I found Mom in the family room fanning herself with a paper plate, the poor person's version of air-conditioning. I wondered how she would react when I told her about the shark attack. Would she still think the beach was a great place to live? Was she already having doubts about living here since a girl had died on the very day of our arrival? Wasn't that a bad omen?

I was beginning to feel like every good thing that happened in my life was automatically followed by fifty bad things. But at least the quota of three deaths had officially been met, satisfying the demands of fate or whatever it was that controlled those kinds of things.

"That poor girl," Mom sighed. "Nobody knows who she is or what happened to her."

Not according to Nevin. He knew what happened, or maybe he was just making a bad joke, I had no idea. "I heard a theory about how she died," I said, picking up a paper plate from the stack. Aunt Emma's house had A/C, but I had been conditioned over many years to fan myself just like Mom. Adjusting the thermostat in summer was still a foreign concept.

"What's the theory? That she drowned?"

"One of the EMTs told me that he thinks a shark killed her."

Mom's brows knit together, and she stopped fanning herself. "A shark?"

"That's what he said, and if that's true, then there's a killer shark out there swimming around in the ocean right behind our house."

"So he thinks Kure Beach is really Amity Island?" she scoffed.

I wouldn't have understood the Amity Island reference, but Mom started joking about the movie *Jaws* soon after she found out we would be living at the beach. When I told her that I didn't want to swim in the ocean because I wasn't a good swimmer, she teased me about being afraid of sharks. I knew she would continue to reference this movie many more times. It obviously hadn't scared her. In fact it had done the opposite.

"So you don't think it's possible that a shark killed her?" I asked.

Mom shrugged, chuckling. "Sharks do live in the ocean, but I highly doubt she was killed by one." She tossed her paper plate through the air like a Frisbee and it landed on the kitchen counter. "Come on. Let's finish exploring the rest of the house. I want to pick out my bedroom." She headed down the hallway, leaving me behind.

I set down the paper plate. The thermostat read seventy-five, but it felt hotter. I wasn't used to the Carolina humidity. I lowered it a couple degrees, hoping the utility bill wouldn't be too high.

Aunt Emma had left us some money, but it was quickly dwindling away. We were living in a multimillion-dollar house and probably only had enough money to last us for the next couple months.

Mom and I had discussed other possible sources of income, wondering how we could afford to live here, and we settled on an idea that we both hoped would work. We decided to rent out two of the bedrooms. I didn't want to live with complete strangers, but it seemed like our best option, especially since Mom wasn't going to work anymore. Like at all.

She said she was going back to college to finally chase her dreams and become some kind of business professional. She'd had a long, colorful mix of dead-end jobs over the years, each one more random than the last. I honestly hoped it would work out for her this time—but deep down, I expected it to go the same way all her other career changes had gone: a big start, then nothing.

I still had a year of high school ahead of me. I didn't know if college was going to be in my future too, but if it was I would need to get a scholarship or apply for grants or something. We had nothing saved up for that, and even if we did, there was another huge expense that couldn't be ignored. Our SUV needed work. A lot of work. It was a miracle we made it all the way here without breaking down. A new car, college tuition, food, utilities, internet, and any other expense would have to be recouped through rental income.

"Winter!" Mom called, her voice brimming with excitement. "You've got to come and see this. Talk about luxury. We don't have to climb the stairs."

Around the corner from the kitchen was an elevator, which I had earlier mistaken for a closet. Mom tried to get me to ride it with her, but I wasn't a fan of tight and confined spaces. "You go ahead," I said. "I'll take the long way."

I climbed all the staircases, stopping to count the bedrooms on each floor. There were eight in total: three on the second floor, three on the third, and two on the fourth. The middle bedroom on the second floor was the one I liked the most. It was located directly at the top of the staircase and had its own bathroom and balcony, a king-size bed, and a walk-in closet. The walls were painted lavender.

Mom stepped out onto the balcony with me. "I knew you would choose this room, because it's purple." She pointed to the balcony on the left. It belonged to the bedroom next to mine. "There's a humongous fireplace in that one. You can see straight through to the bathroom, which means I can enjoy a fire while I'm either soaking in the tub or lying in bed. I swear I've died and gone to heaven, Winter."

Mom continued to ramble on about her new bedroom. I told her how much I liked mine, but what neither of us talked about was Aunt Emma's bedroom. It was also located on this floor. All of her things were still in there. I didn't go inside to look around. I just peeked in and then shut the door.

"I think my room needs to be brightened up," she said. "It's too drab and lifeless. Maybe some colorful throw pillows might help. Definitely some new curtains."

We didn't have the extra money to purchase those things. I reminded her of this, and she ignored me. Mom had never been good with money, which meant that I had to be the responsible one.

Mom and I finished touring the rest of the house, and then we went back downstairs. She sat on the couch to relax, and I headed out onto the back deck.

I gazed out at the beach behind our house. Just over the dunes, I could clearly see the crowd. It had dwindled in size, but the number of first responders had increased. Four-wheel-drive vehicles surrounded the scene. I wondered how much longer they were going to be there.

Down the stairs and through the backyard, I made my way to the rear gate, resting my elbows on it. My attention shifted to the lifeguard tower. Jaxson and Eli were still there. I truly did want to ask them about the dead girl, wondering if they would confirm what Nevin had said. Both Eli and Jaxson had seen the girl up close and were likely the ones who pulled her out of the ocean.

I thought about how irritated Eli got when Jaxson asked him if he had ever seen a dead body before. That was a stupid and insensitive question to ask. Eli seemed truly bothered about what had happened to the girl. I wondered if he tried to revive her. Eli probably fulfilled all of his job responsibilities, while Jaxson probably stood there and watched. Or maybe I was being too critical of Jaxson. I knew I shouldn't judge him, since I didn't have all the facts. Maybe Jaxson did try to save the girl, and he was upset about what happened. Maybe he just handled stress differently, kind of like Mom. She was more of a suffer-in-silence type of person. She could put on a fake smile, fooling almost anybody.

Mom usually pretended like life was great, even when it wasn't. Even after the most horrific tragedy of our lives, she managed to pretend. My memories of that day were kind of splotchy since I was only ten, but I still remember some things quite clearly. There were four of us at home when it happened: Mom, Aunt Emma, me, and my baby brother, Kyle.

I remember the sound of Aunt Emma's scream. It cut through the house like a siren and jolted me awake. I sat up in bed, confused, my heart thudding before I even knew why. Something in me already knew it was bad.

I followed the sound of crying. Mom was kneeling on the floor near the crib, rocking Kyle back and forth in her arms. She was sobbing so hard she couldn't breathe right. Aunt Emma was just standing there, staring at them.

They didn't notice me at first. I hovered in the doorway, silent. I don't think I really understood what was going on. I wanted Mom to say something, but she wouldn't even look at me.

When the ambulance came, flashing lights lit up the walls, but no one was moving fast. It was too late. I remember staring at Kyle's blanket, the one with little ducks on it, lying on the floor. Nobody picked it up.

The yelling came later. That *wasn't* new. Mom and Aunt Emma argued all the time, but that day was different. It wasn't loud in the same way—it was meaner. Sharper.

Mom pointed at Aunt Emma, trembling. "It's your fault."

"My fault?" Aunt Emma gasped.

"You didn't put Kyle to bed on his back like I told you to."

"How dare you blame me for this? You should have checked on him when he started crying in the middle of the night."

Out of the three people I loved the most, Kyle was gone, and if this fighting didn't stop, I feared I would lose Aunt Emma too.

Soon my fear became a reality.

Mom started pulling away too. She was there, but yet she wasn't. Something in her had shifted. She didn't talk to me as much, not in the same way. She wasn't angry, exactly—just far away. Aunt Emma tried to fill in the gaps, but it was never the same. I think they both broke that day in different ways. And I was just there to watch the cracks form.

There was no funeral. Mom went back to her cashier job at the hardware store, just like it was another normal day. She never cried again over Kyle, at least not in front of me. It was like she was living in some kind of pretend world, as if Kyle never existed.

After Aunt Emma moved out, I never saw her again.

I wiped a tear off my cheek and blinked my eyes to stop them from blurring, then I stared at the ocean. I stood there for a long time, until I felt calm again.

When I turned around, my heart leaped in my chest. There was a guy with dark hair, orange shorts, and no shirt lying on a lounge chair in the backyard of the coral-colored house. A large German shepherd roamed around the yard sniffing at the bushes. I could see just about every square inch of the next-door neighbor's backyard through the wrought iron fences, which meant that he could see me too.

Goose bumps pricked my arms when he turned his head toward me. Was this the same person who had been watching Mom and me from the upstairs window earlier? Was he watching me now from behind his dark sunglasses?

I turned around so quickly, I almost tripped over my own feet. Half walking, half running, my nerves drawn taut, I raced through the backyard, past the firepit, the outdoor kitchen, the hammock, and the lounge chairs, straight up to the deck.

I avoided looking in his direction even though I could feel him staring at me. When I finally reached the inside of the house, I locked the sliding glass door and drew the curtains shut.

I paced the floor in the family room until I calmed down enough to slow my breathing. What was with this neighbor? Was he always going to be watching me every time I went outside? I hadn't even moved my stuff in yet and already he had spied on me in the front yard and now in the back. He was watching me coming and going. It was too creepy.

Maybe I wouldn't have felt so on edge if it hadn't been for what I had gone through six months ago. I still had terrible nightmares about what happened to my friend Venus and her siblings. I had ignored clear warning signs from her boyfriend Chaz, and said nothing. I never wanted to make that mistake again.

I headed to the kitchen and poured myself a glass of cold water. I leaned back against the counter, soaking in my surroundings: stainless steel appliances, a double oven, a huge gas stove, a center island with a second sink. I wondered if Mom would actually cook since we had such an amazing kitchen. Maybe I would try to cook more too.

Feeling a lot less anxious now, I set my glass down on the counter, wondering what I should do next. Mom and I still needed to unload the trailer and bring our stuff inside. If we waited much longer, we would both probably be too tired to do it. The cross-country trip had already exhausted us.

Heading back up the stairs, I found Mom sitting on her bed with her phone. The smile on her face revealed to me what she was up to. My mood immediately darkened. I knew she was texting Fred. We had talked about him many times during the drive here, and she promised me that she was done with him.

Mom and Fred were not good for each other. They both liked to spend money way too much. He would borrow money and never pay it back. Sometimes he would steal it. He spent time in prison for embezzlement. I didn't want him anywhere near us. It was an absolute miracle that I managed to convince Mom to leave him behind. She needed to forget about him. Why was she so weak when it came to men? I never met my dad, or Kyle's. At least not that I knew of. But among the many who had come and gone, I knew this much: I hated Fred.

I cleared my throat and crossed my arms, leaning against the doorframe. "Please tell me you're not texting *him*."

Mom's lips pursed together as she shot me an irritated look. She slid her phone into her pocket. "He just wanted to know if we made it here safely."

"Sure he did, and I bet he also wanted to know when he could move in. You cannot let that happen."

Mom let out an exasperated sigh as she buried her face in her hands. "You don't understand what it's like for me. I'm not getting any younger. I don't turn heads like I used to, and I'm afraid I'm not going to find anybody else who will love me."

I had already tried to boost Mom's self-esteem thousands of times before. I would tell her that she was beautiful, that she was smart and kind. I would tell her that she deserved to be loved and respected and that she would find a good man who would treat her right one day. But no matter how many times I told her these things, I couldn't make her believe it.

If she let Fred back into our lives right now, I was sure he would mismanage her money and cause us to lose this house. We were going to have a tough enough time as it was and didn't need him around to complicate things. Maybe I needed to be more harsh with Mom. Would she listen to me then?

"Mom. Do I need to remind you that Fred never paid you back any of the money he borrowed from you? Do I need to remind you that he bought a car using your credit and didn't make any payments? He's rude and mean, and he treats you like garbage. Fred doesn't love you."

She held up her hand, metal bracelets clanging together. "Fine. Okay. I hear you. I'll stop texting him," she huffed, leaving the room.

That's what she told me last time.

I headed back downstairs, following after her.

She went straight to the kitchen. "I'm craving chocolate." She started looking through the cupboards and drawers. "That's weird. There isn't any food in here."

I walked over to the pantry to look inside. The shelves were bare. Then I opened the refrigerator. "The only thing in here is a box of baking soda."

Mom slammed another cupboard shut. "I guess we can order pizza for dinner."

I nodded in agreement. "And we still have some snacks and drinks left over in the SUV. We should probably bring that stuff in."

Mom let out a heavy sigh. "All right. Let's get it over with."

Unloading the trailer and bringing our things inside wasn't as bad as I thought it would be, thanks to the elevator. I carried our things in from the car. Mom took them up the elevator and delivered them to our bedrooms.

We mostly brought smaller items like clothes, shoes, books, and keepsakes. All of our belongings could have fit snugly inside the SUV, but Mom insisted on bringing her china hutch, so we had to rent a small trailer.

This piece of furniture was massive, ugly, and way too heavy for us to carry inside on our own. Fred had given it to her, which was another reason why I didn't like it. Fred probably found it on the side of the road somewhere, and that's where it belonged, not inside our beautiful new home.

"You do know we're probably going to drop this monstrosity, don't you?" I warned her. "And then it will officially be a piece of junk. We'll have to throw it away, or burn it." In my opinion, burning it sounded like the best option, and there was a firepit in the backyard just waiting for such an occasion.

Mom wiped the sweat from her forehead as she looked out toward the street. A man riding a beat-up old bicycle, holding a partially wrapped bottle of booze in one hand, was passing by the front of our house. He was obviously intoxicated, barely able to stay upright on his bike.

Mom pointed. "What about asking him to help?"

"Are you kidding me? No."

She scratched her head, then her eyes settled on the coral-colored house. "Let's ask our new neighbors."

The cold, dreadful feeling I had experienced earlier returned again. "No way! Somebody in that house has been watching us all day. I don't want to invite a creeper or a murderer into our lives."

"A murderer?" Mom scoffed. "Don't be ridiculous." She headed toward the house, skirt flying.

I darted in front of her, blocking her path. "Mom. I'm being serious. I've got a really bad feeling. We should not go there. Let's just leave the china hutch on the curb with a sign that says 'free.' It's not going to match the furniture in the house anyway."

"We're keeping it." Mom grabbed my shoulders, pushing me aside.

I followed after her. We needed to stick together—it would be safer that way. And I wanted to make sure that she didn't go inside.

My stomach twisted and turned as Mom rang the doorbell. What if our neighbor was the next Jeffrey Dahmer or Ted Bundy? Before my thoughts could continue down that dark road any further, the door started to open. I held my breath.

Standing directly in front of us was that same guy I had

seen in the backyard. His shoulders were broad, hands large enough to strangle someone's neck. I was sure of it. His mouth was set in a firm straight line, far from a welcoming smile. He still had on dark sunglasses, which made him look even more mysterious and frightening. But up close I could see he was young. Was he my age, I wondered. Would he be going to school with me? What kind of reputation did he have? Was he a loner? Was he someone who got into trouble all the time? Maybe he was a charmer with a secret desire for murder.

"Hi there," Mom said. "We're your new neighbors. I'm Sasha Covington, and this is my daughter, Winter." The German shepherd suddenly appeared, poking its nose out the door. Luckily it didn't bark or snarl at us. Mom motioned toward our trailer. "We have this incredibly heavy china hutch that we need to unload. Do you think you could help us carry it inside?"

The thought of this guy entering our house made my heart hammer in my chest.

"Sure," he replied, reaching for something. When I saw what was in his hand, I wondered if this was his attempt at a joke. I didn't see the humor in it at all.

"You're blind?" Mom blurted out, staring at the cane in his hand.

"That's what the doctors tell me," he replied with a crooked grin.

Then it all connected in my head: his dark sunglasses, the German shepherd, and of course his cane.

Mom and I exchanged surprised looks.

She clasped her hand over her chest. "I'm so sorry. I didn't mean to blurt that out like that."

"Don't worry about it. I get that kind of reaction all the time." He stepped out onto the porch with us, the german shepherd right behind him. "Stay Max." he said, nudging the dog back inside.

Mom held up her hands, motioning for him to stop, as if that would make a difference. "You don't have to help us. We can go ask another neighbor."

"You can certainly do that if you want, but I don't mind helping. Just don't put me in the front. I'm a much better follower." He smiled again with his crooked grin.

It took me a moment to regain my composure. My mind was still reeling over the fact that our neighbor wasn't a murderer. He couldn't have been. He was blind. What were Mom and I doing? We were about to make a blind person come over and help us move our furniture. This could not happen. I mouthed the word "no" to Mom.

She shrugged her shoulders in response. "Well," she said to him. "If you're sure that you're okay with this."

"I'm sure, if you're sure."

Mom watched intently as he walked toward the steps. "Do you need help?"

He chuckled. "No. I've got these memorized."

What in the world were we doing? We should have never come here. But I couldn't stop the train wreck from happening. All I could do was go along and hope for the best. I decided that I would just act like this was all normal; we're normal, he's normal. Yeah, right. Who was I kidding?

I glared at Mom, shaking my head, before approaching our neighbor. "Uh, thank you for helping us."

"Yeah, no problem. Oh. I forgot to introduce myself. My name's Hunter. Hunter Lee."

"It's so nice to meet you, Hunter." Mom smiled, reaching to shake his hand, which he didn't shake because he couldn't see it.

"Are you here for the summer?" he asked.

"We'll be living here forever," I replied.

"That's right," Mom said. "Winter will be starting her senior year of high school this fall."

"Nice," Hunter replied, holding out his arm. "So where's this furniture that you need help moving?"

Mom nudged me over to him, so I took hold of his arm. He smelled like Axe body spray, but the scent wasn't too overpowering. I felt a little uncomfortable being so close to him since we just met. But he seemed like a nice guy. He couldn't have been the same person I saw in the window earlier. That had to have been somebody else.

We were able to lift the china hutch and take it into the house without any problems. Hunter didn't seem to struggle at all under the weight and took most of it upon himself.

"Would you like to stay for a drink?" Mom asked.

I usually watched people's facial expressions and paid close attention to their eyes, but I couldn't see Hunter's eyes at all. I couldn't see his eyebrows either. His sunglasses were too big and dark. I had no idea if he was even remotely interested in staying for a drink. His expression seemed blank.

"You don't have to stay if you don't want to," I said. "We kind of showed up unannounced, and we don't want to keep you if you were in the middle of something."

"Yeah, I probably better get going. I bet y'all have a lot of unpacking to do." The corner of his mouth turned down, and I knew I messed up. He wanted to stay.

"You know," I quickly added. "We'll actually be unpacking for days, so we'd love for you to hang out for a little while, if you're available."

"Okay." He shrugged. "Maybe for a little bit."

Mom began unpacking a box of old dishes, placing them inside the ugly china hutch.

"Do you want to go into the kitchen?" I asked him.

"Sure. Wherever is fine with me."

"So, um..." I hesitated. "How does this work? Should I..."

He smiled with his crooked grin again. "I promise that I won't get the wrong idea if you hold my arm."

I linked my arm around his, feeling slightly embarrassed, wishing I hadn't hesitated. I directed Hunter to a stool at the kitchen counter and grabbed a Pepsi from the ice chest. Most of the ice had melted from our trip, but the drinks were still cold. I popped open my can, then his, instantly realizing it was probably really dumb of me to open it for him. I grabbed another can and set it on the counter in front of him. "Here you go."

"Thanks." He reached out and grabbed hold of it on the first try, then popped it open.

I wondered how he was able to appear so perfectly put together since he couldn't see his reflection in the mirror. It probably helped that he kept his hair cut short. His face was clean-shaven, and his unwrinkled T-shirt was white, so it didn't clash with his orange shorts.

If I were blind, I would look like a sea monster. My hair would have a ton of flyaways, as if I had stuck my finger in a light socket. And I was certain that Mom would dress me in overly matchy clothes like we were twins. The whole image was terrifying.

Hunter set the can down on the counter, keeping his hand on it. "So is it just the two of you living here?"

"Yep. Just me and my mom." My gaze shifted to the window. The sky was a beautiful swirl of deep purples and blues.

"That's cool. Where'd you move from?"

I told him about living in Utah and how freezing cold it would get during the winter. He preferred living in warmer climates, having lived in New Mexico, California, and Texas. But he was originally from Kure Beach and had just recently moved back.

"So when did you move in?" I asked.

"A week ago."

I was disappointed to learn that Hunter had moved in after

Aunt Emma died. It would have been nice to talk to someone who had known her. I had so many questions about her life. What kinds of things did she enjoy doing? Did she have any friends? Did she have favorite places she would go to hang out? What had she been doing all these years? Mr. Davis didn't have much to say about her. She was just another one of his clients, and he seemed like a busy man.

Hunter and I continued to talk for a while, mostly about the places we used to live. I was kind of hoping that he would tell me about his disability, but he didn't. I was curious to find out if he had been born blind, or if something had caused him to lose his sight later in life, like an illness or an accident. Would it be rude if I asked? Probably.

He swiveled back and forth in his chair. "If you ever want me to show you around Kure, I'd be happy to take you on a tour."

"Thanks," I replied, trying to sound like I believed him even though I wondered if he was just teasing. How in the world could he take me on a tour?

I took a sip of my soda, then realized I hadn't seen Mom in a while. Where did she disappear to? Was she talking to Fred on the phone and trying to hide it from me?

Hunter set his can down on the counter. The clinking sound revealed that it was empty.

"Want another one?" I asked.

"No, I'm good."

I picked up his can, and as I walked across the kitchen, from the corner of my eye I saw Hunter slowly turning his head like he was watching me. The lid of the trash can flopped back down, and when I turned around, Hunter's head was facing forward again. Just how blind was he? That was a question I wasn't sure I should ask him, not yet anyway.

I sat at the counter, directly across from him, my attention solely focused on his sunglasses. I wished I could see his eyes and the direction they were looking.

Since Hunter seemed to be an expert about Kure Beach, I wondered if he could tell me more about the kinds of things that typically happened here. Were shark attacks the norm? "A girl died on the beach earlier. Did you hear about it?" The image of her dead body covered in a white sheet flashed through my mind.

"Yeah, I heard about that on the news."

He did? Great. This was perfect. I couldn't wait to find out what they had said. "So are shark attacks a frequent occurrence around here?"

"She was attacked by a shark?" he asked. "That's not what they said on the news."

"Oh," I replied, feeling kind of stupid. How could I have been so gullible? Nevin had either been lying to me or he was teasing. What a jerk. "What did they say on the news?"

"They didn't say how she died. They didn't mention her name or much else, really. They just said that a female had died here on the beach."

Okay, so maybe a shark attack was still a possibility. Maybe Nevin wasn't teasing me.

Hunter picked up his cane, rising from his chair. "I should probably head on home since it's getting late."

Already? But I still wanted to find out who that was in the upstairs window of his house. Was it his brother, his father, an uncle? Hunter seemed like he was in a hurry.

"Do you mind if I go through the backyard?" he asked.

I linked my arm around his, guiding him along the way. The fences bordering our yards were black wrought iron, about four feet high, with gates directly across from each other. A walkway ran between our fences, providing a pathway to the beach.

"It was nice talking to you, Hunter."

He turned his head to face me but was off by a few inches. "I'm usually home, so feel free to stop by whenever."

"Okay, sure. And same to you. Come back over sometime."

Hunter continued along the cement walkway toward his house, not really using his cane. He moved so swiftly, as if he had done it hundreds of times before, which seemed strange since he hadn't lived there that long. Again, I was questioning just how blind he was. Surely he wouldn't be faking, would he? Only a truly disturbed person would pretend to be blind. Hunter didn't seem like that.

After he disappeared into his house, my attention turned to the beach. Since the sun hadn't fully set yet, I decided to walk down the path to the water's edge before it got too dark. All of the people were gone now: the police, the emergency responders, the lifeguards. The beach had a calm and peaceful feeling to it, as if nothing bad had ever happened there today. But still, the memory of that girl's dead body remained present in my mind.

I stood in front of the ocean, just out of its reach, wondering if there was a killer shark out there somewhere. Had it already moved on or was it a local?

My eyes squinted, straining to see. There was something moving out there, gliding along the choppy water. Was it a pelican floating, waiting to catch a fish? Was it a shark? I dared not take another step closer, but rather focused my gaze. The sky had dimmed, and I struggled to make out the figure. There! Wait. No, it wasn't the dorsal fin of a shark. It was a person swimming. Why would anyone ever choose to swim by themselves so far away from shore?

Turning to my right, I spotted a man in the distance, walking in my direction. It seemed odd that he would be wearing long sleeves and long pants and have a hood pulled up over his head in this kind of heat. The cold ocean water suddenly swept over my feet, and so did an uneasy feeling, which I took as a sign that I should hurry back to the house.

CHAPTER 7

TAMARA (BELLANY)

The cops were still searching for me, but they were never going to find me.

After I left Washington, I spent some time in North Dakota. I rented a cabin and laid low for several weeks.

I chose that little town because the old lady who had sat next to me on the bus got off at that stop. She seemed like the type I could take advantage of: vulnerable, overly trusting, and just gullible enough not to see it coming. But she didn't have anything worth taking.

I knew my next target had to check the same boxes—plus one more: They had to be rich. Without that, it wasn't worth the risk.

I needed a way to screen potential marks more easily, so I got a job waitressing at a little restaurant in town. The owner, Mr. Vickers, believed my story—the same one I had used back in Washington. I told him that I had left an abusive boyfriend and was worried he might track me down and kill me. I showed him photos that I had downloaded from the internet showing bruised arms and ribs. "That's what my ex did to me," I said, acting like I was on the verge of tears. So Mr. Vickers understood when I asked to be paid in cash, off the books.

After weeks of coming up empty, I figured it was time to move on. That's when I decided to tag along with that same old woman from the bus. Her name was Martha. I had stayed friendly with her, mostly because I hoped it might eventually lead me to some kind of money. She mentioned she was planning another visit to see her son in New York. That piqued my interest. I told her I had always dreamed of seeing the city, but never had the chance. That was a lie. I had been to New York several times.

Just as we were about to get off the bus, Martha took hold of my hand, pulling me back to my seat. "I'm glad you decided to leave North Dakota," she said in her tiny, frail voice. "It wasn't safe for you to stay there. Your ex-boyfriend had tracked you down."

My hand tightened around hers. What was she talking about? Had someone come looking for me? I knew that Martha sometimes told me the same stories over and over again and that her memory wasn't the best, but her stories never had anything to do with me until now.

Martha leaned in close to whisper in my ear, even though

nobody could hear her. The entire bus was empty. "Don't worry. He won't bother you."

"What happened? Did you talk to him?" I asked, wondering if I should be concerned or if this was just a figment of her imagination. I couldn't be too careful. There were people out there making it their mission to hunt me down. Martha might have been telling me the truth.

My eyes scanned the windows. Were there cops waiting outside? Were they going to arrest me as soon as I stepped off the bus? Martha still hadn't answered my questions. "Martha," I said, my voice stern. "Tell me what happened."

She smiled, a devious twinkle in her eye. "He said his name was TJ. Or was it CJ? Yes, I think it was CJ." She placed her hand on top of her head. "He wore a cowboy hat and boots. He said he's been looking for you, showed me a picture of you." She pointed at me. "Your hair was much darker in the picture, almost black, but I knew it was you."

Hearing her describe my previous hair color confirmed that she had actually met someone who was looking for me, but I had no idea who CJ was. He could have been an FBI agent, a detective, or a private investigator. He could have been anybody from my past, using a fake name.

Whoever he was, I needed to know how he managed to track me down. Had I messed up somewhere? Had I overlooked something? But I couldn't think about those things now. None of that would matter if I got caught. "You didn't tell CJ that I was living there, did you?" Please don't say that you did. Please be smarter than that, you stupid old lady.

Martha's eyes shifted to the right as she searched her memory. "Well... I told him that I had seen you and that you were headed up north to Canada." She giggled, patting my hand. "I know how to tell a good lie when I want to. You don't need to worry about him, my dear. He's long gone now."

If only it was that simple.

I asked her to describe what he looked like, but she wasn't able to provide me with anything useful. She couldn't recall his hair or eye color. When she said that he was probably 6'10" or 6'12" I stopped asking her questions. She was no help.

Just before Martha exited the bus, she turned back to face me. "Oh. I forgot. He called you Charity."

Hearing that name again sent a surge of anger through me. I had been so close to having everything when I was Charity: the perfect life, money, and Roy. Too bad Roy will never meet his real mother, but that's what he gets for choosing Samantha over me.

As soon as I got off the bus, I made a beeline for the nearest store. I changed my clothes in the bathroom, put on a different hat, and exited through the back door.

Whoever was after me was getting too close. I decided I was going to have to make some drastic changes.

CHAPTER 8

WINTER

The next morning, I made a quick trip to the grocery store while Mom slept in. By the time she came downstairs, I had already put away the groceries and finished typing up an ad to rent out two of our bedrooms. "How does this look?" I asked, turning the screen of my laptop toward Mom.

She shot me a questioning look. "You think we can really charge that much for rent?"

"I researched it first. This is the going rate for someone to rent a room on the beach." I felt confident I had priced it right.

Mom made a face like she didn't believe me. "Well, if we don't get any responses, then we'll know we're asking too much."

I turned the screen back to face me and clicked the button to post it. "If we get two renters, and keep them, we should be able to afford to live here."

The teakettle whistled. Mom sighed, getting up from her chair.

I placed a carton of milk and a box of cereal on the table, wondering if I was correct to assume that two renters would bring in enough money. Maybe we needed three. But I didn't like the idea of having three strangers live here. Two was already enough to give me an ulcer. I had no idea what kind of people would want to rent a room from us. Hopefully we would get lucky, and this would be a good experience. But who was I kidding? I had never been lucky before.

Mom dropped a packet of herbal tea into her mug and joined me at the table. "As soon as we get some renters, I need to purchase a more reliable vehicle."

The SUV hadn't broken down yet, so a new car wasn't an urgent need. "Aren't we going to wait and see how high the utility bill is each month first? Our bank balance is really low, especially now that your college tuition has been paid." I cringed hearing myself talk like this. Didn't parents usually say these things to their children, not the other way around? I really wished Mom was better with money.

She continued to rattle off her long and expensive wish list, which included a new wardrobe, a new phone, and a new computer.

I wanted some new things too, but I was going to be patient. I pointed at Mom with a serious look on my face. "Before you get a phone, I'm going to get a phone."

Mom had the nerve to start lecturing me about taking

better care of my things. As if she could talk. She was the irresponsible one. But I had made one mistake, and she wasn't going to let me forget it. I had set my phone on the roof of the car during our trip here. Yep, it went bye-bye.

If I really wanted to, I could go purchase a cheap phone right now, just something to get by until I could afford one that I really wanted. But I wasn't in a hurry. I didn't have anybody to text or call anyway, not since Chaz lied to the police about me.

He told the cops that I was his accomplice, which was a huge lie. I had no idea that he was going to kill Venus and her two siblings. But being accused was just as bad as being guilty. When people at school heard about this, I became public enemy number two. People who I thought were my friends weren't really my friends after all. Every one of them turned on me.

In order to avoid being harassed online, I had to unplug from all social media. I ended up dropping out of school too. I should have graduated a few weeks ago, only I didn't have enough credits. So I was going to be jumping into the pool of seniors again when the new school year started in the fall. Mom suggested going the GED route like she did, but I thought having a diploma might be helpful on scholarship applications.

I poured some milk onto my cereal and took a bite much sooner than I should have. The cereal hadn't softened yet and was a struggle to swallow.

Mom rested her chin on her hand. "I wish I could go out to the beach with you today, but I've got to go purchase my textbooks and tour the college campus."

"I don't think I'll get a chance to go out to the beach today," I said, hoping she would realize that she wasn't going to be missing out on anything. "I'm probably going to spend most of the day unpacking."

Mom dumped a spoonful of sugar over her cereal and into her tea. "If you get done unpacking your stuff, feel free to move on to mine. I've got homework assignments to catch up on."

"Don't worry. I'll take care of it." I already planned on unpacking her things. I didn't want her to get distracted from her college work. Earning a degree would be so good for Mom. I was sure this would help give her some more self-confidence. Maybe she would even start dating better men. We didn't need Fred showing up here, or any of his clones.

Over the next couple of days, I spent most of my time organizing, unpacking, and cleaning the house. As soon as all of those things were finished, I headed out to the beach so I could work on my tan, even though I wasn't sure if that was even possible. But I figured I needed to at least give it a shot.

I walked past those same two lifeguards who had been on duty the day that girl died. Jaxson was once again blowing bubbles with bright green gum, staring down at his phone. Eli was sitting next to him, his attention focused on the ocean, watching the swimmers. I wondered how Eli managed to tolerate Jaxson.

I made sure to find a spot on the beach far away from where that girl's dead body had laid. The wind blew my towel over several times, so I piled some sand onto the corners to weigh it down. Then a seagull targeted me in search of food, but that bird was out of luck. I didn't bring any snacks with me.

After the sun beat down on my front and my back for a decent amount of time, I decided I should probably head back inside. As I walked past the lifeguard tower, I glanced over my shoulder and saw both lifeguards craning their necks to look at me. The warmth in my cheeks intensified. I wanted Eli to notice me, but now I felt self-conscious. Maybe they were both looking at me because my skin was so pale, but then again, it might have been for some other reason equally embarrassing. I shrugged the towel off my shoulders and wrapped it around my waist to cover up. My bathing suit was riding up, and I didn't want to pull out my wedgie right in front of them.

Just before I reached the back gate, I turned and looked again, trying to act casual. Disappointment hit when I saw that only Jaxson was still watching me. He didn't look away even when our eyes met. I almost shot him a dirty look but then a memory of Venus surfaced in my mind.

We had been arguing over something stupid and she said, "Whenever you deliberately try to look irritated with somebody, it comes across as if you're psycho or something. Trust me, you really shouldn't do it."

Her words stung at first, but after the initial shock wore off, I did a little more self-analysis, wondering if maybe she was right. Did I look like a psycho? And what did a psycho actually look like?

At school, I wasn't part of the rich, popular clique. I was part of the poor clique. We were known as the mean girls. The rich clique had plenty of mean girls too, yet for some reason they didn't have the same stigma.

Venus was the leader of the mean girls. She had a bad attitude and a smart mouth and dished out plenty of irritated, dirty looks on a daily basis. She didn't hold back when it came to sharing her true feelings and opinions. She was a critical person, judgmental, and skilled at tearing people down emotionally. She was a role model who other haters looked up to. She was feared and respected. So when Chaz accused me of being his accomplice in the murders of Venus and her younger brother and sister, all of my fellow hater friends turned on me, viciously.

Moving here to Kure Beach and getting away from all of my former so-called friends was probably the best chance I had at finding happiness again and living a normal life. I didn't want to ruin it. Instead of jumping into the default mode of being a hater girl, I was going to try to be a little more selective and careful about when and to whom I dished out dirty looks.

As I walked through the backyard, I remembered that I needed to pull the garbage can to the curb for trash day, so I headed around to the side of the house and wheeled it out to the front.

"Hey," a deep voice called. I turned around and saw some guy wearing dark sunglasses and a baseball cap. He had just pulled Hunter's garbage can to the curb. "Remember me?" he asked.

The hat and sunglasses covered up his face too much. I wasn't sure if I recognized him.

Then he pulled his sunglasses off, revealing his dark brown eyes and pale, almost invisible eyebrows. "Does this help?" he asked.

I recognized him now. It was Nevin, the EMT who told me about the shark attack. It was difficult for me not to stare at his muscular shoulders and arms. His shirt had covered them up before, but now he was wearing a tank top. "Yeah, I remember you. Do you live with Hunter?"

Nevin's smile widened, exposing his teeth, then he quickly adjusted back to a half smile. I got the impression that he was trying to hide his crooked teeth. They really weren't that bad-looking, though. "I don't live here," he said. "I help Hunter. I'm his personal assistant."

"Oh. So you have two jobs."

Nevin rested his elbow on the garbage can. "Yep. But working for Hunter doesn't really feel like work. We're friends. He and I used to hang out when we were kids." Nevin almost smiled again, but then he forced his lips back closed. "Did you just move in?"

"Yeah, about a week after Hunter did."

He nodded and there were a few beats of silence. "Well, if you want, I can bring your trash can out every week when I take out Hunter's."

I didn't feel comfortable asking him to do that. "No, that's okay. I don't mind doing it."

Nevin's eyes traveled over to the driveway. "Is that your Explorer?"

"Yeah." Why did he want to know? Was it so he could laugh about what a piece of junk it was?

"I was just about to wash Hunter's dune buggy. I can come over and wash your car after I'm done." He shrugged. "I'll have all the stuff out anyway."

The Explorer hadn't been washed since we arrived here. It definitely looked filthy. I shook my head. Why was he offering in the first place? Did he just enjoy washing cars? Or did he want an excuse to hang out with me?

"I'm not gonna ask you to pay me to do it," he added with a chuckle.

What a weird thing to say. Now this whole thing felt even more awkward. "No, I don't need you to wash it. I'll get around to it soon."

"Are you sure?"

"Yeah, I'm sure."

Nevin's phone started chiming in his pocket, and I was

glad for the interruption. I took a step back and said, "See ya around," hoping he would get the hint that I wasn't interested in continuing our conversation.

"Hey, I don't know your name."

I turned around but kept walking backward. "My name's Winter."

His phone continued to chime. "I'm Nevin."

"I know. I read it on your name tag the day we met."

He almost smiled again as he placed his phone to his ear.

Once I got back inside the house I headed straight to the bathroom, wondering if I had tanned at all or if my skin was still embarrassingly pale.

When the light flicked on, and I saw my reflection in the mirror, my stomach dropped. I pushed the strap off my shoulder, confirming just how bad it looked. My skin was bright red. I continued to examine myself. Even the tops of my ears and the part in my hair were sunburned. I looked like a lobster.

As the day progressed, the pain got worse. I was miserable. Anything that touched my skin felt like sandpaper—no, it felt like shards of glass.

I didn't go back out to the beach for several days after that, not until my sunburn went away. And each time I did, I made sure not to stay too long. I had learned my lesson.

Sometimes when I was out there, I would see the same people lounging around, tanning their already overly tanned bodies. There were also a lot of people who were unfamiliar, probably there just for the day or the weekend.

The two guys that I saw almost every day were the lifeguards, Eli and Jaxson. They never spoke to me, and I never spoke to them. I kept my distance, making sure I was close enough to watch and observe them now and then, and at the same time far enough away so that I wouldn't come off as being some kind of stalker.

The same thing always happened. As I left the beach to walk back to my house, I would glance over my shoulder and catch both of them staring at me. Yes, even Eli. I was glad he had noticed me. But I was beginning to wonder if he would ever come and talk to me. I didn't want to be the one to initiate a conversation. What would I even say? Anything I could think of just sounded awkward and lame. I hoped the whole summer wouldn't go on like this.

When I was about to walk inside the house, I saw Hunter in his backyard. He was standing there while his dog Max wandered around the yard peeing.

"Hunter," I called.

He approached the gate. "Hey, Winter. Are you busy? Do you want to hang out?"

"I'm not busy. I just got back from the beach." I helped him through the backyard and led him over to one of the lounge chairs. Max sat down at his feet.

Nevin pushed a lawn mower into his backyard. He waved at me, and I waved back, then he started up the lawn mower.

Nevin was wearing a baseball cap again, dark sunglasses, and was shirtless. Even from several yards away, I could see his six-pack abs.

"I met Nevin the other day," I said. "How old is he?" I wondered if I would be going to school with him.

"He's nineteen. He graduated from high school last year." Hunter waved his hand in front of his face as a fly buzzed by.

I thought about my conversation with Nevin and how he referred to Hunter as his childhood friend. "How well do you know Nevin?"

"We used to hang out all the time when we were kids."

"So did you stay in touch even after you moved away?"

"No, not really, but he's still the same as he was before." Hunter swatted at another fly. "We ran into each other at the grocery store a day or two after I moved here. My mom's the one who recognized him. We got to talking, and I found out that he was tired of working at the grocery store. He wanted to find another job, and I still hadn't found anybody to hire as my personal assistant, so things worked out for both of us."

I was about to ask him another question about Nevin, but he started talking first. "So where's your dad?"

"No idea. I've never met the man."

Hunter cocked his head. "Why is that?"

"He left my mom before I was born, and he has never tried to get in contact with me." If he was anything like the other losers Mom had dated in the past, I didn't want anything to do with him. "Are your parents still married?"

"Yeah, but I don't talk to my dad. He was abusive and had a terrible temper. I don't talk to my brother either. He's just like my dad."

"That must have really sucked growing up with two people like that living under the same roof as you," I said, watching Max roll over and close his eyes.

"Yeah, I couldn't wait to move into this house and be on my own."

"You mean to tell me that you live in that huge house by yourself?"

He draped his arm over the back of his chair and crossed his leg. "I'm eighteen. I took my GED two years ago and graduated early."

My focus shifted to his enormous house. I wondered if he was the one who had been standing in the upstairs window the day Mom and I moved in. It couldn't have been Nevin since he was working his EMT job that day. Maybe Hunter was just standing there enjoying the warmth of the sun. I couldn't think of any other reason why he'd hover in the window like that.

As I stared at Hunter's dark sunglasses, unable to see his eyes, I wondered how an abusive father, who he didn't speak to anymore, could financially support him and buy him such an expensive house. Was it because his father was so filthy rich that the extra expense didn't matter? Or did Hunter work from home and make his own money? What kind of job did he do? "How can you afford to live in that house by yourself?"

Another fly buzzed by his face, but he didn't swat at it. "I came into some money…unexpectedly."

Oh. He must have inherited his house from a rich relative like Mom and I did. "If my aunt hadn't left us this house in her will, my mom and I would never be able to afford to live here."

He nodded, then crossed his other leg. "Do you have any other family living here in North Carolina?"

"It's just me and my mom."

He uncrossed his leg, sitting forward. "I thought I heard a man's voice the other day, coming from your front yard. Who was that?"

Mom and I had interviewed a renter. Maybe that's who he heard. "Tim Woods. He's going to rent one of our bedrooms."

That same fly came buzzing by Hunter again. This time he smacked at it hard. "I know Tim," he said, his lips contorted like he was either mad at the fly or mad at the world, I didn't know which.

"Oh really?"

"My dad hired him to do some remodeling on our house years ago. His workers did a shoddy job, and then they lied about it." Hunter shook his head, his neck reddening. "Tim is as crooked as they come. Be careful. He might try to swindle you and your mom out of rent money, and I wouldn't hire him to do any repair work on your house, unless you want it done wrong."

Tim had told us that he worked construction, and I knew

this was true, because I had seen him installing the back fence at a neighbor's house. During our interview, I kept staring at his gory shark tattoo and at his mullet. But other than that, he seemed normal. He paid his rent in advance, and Mom seemed to really like him. "Thanks for the warning."

Hunter strummed his fingers on the arm of the chair, looking agitated.

"Are you thirsty?" I asked. "Want a Pepsi?"

"Yeah, that'd be great."

I went to the bathroom first, then grabbed a couple cold cans of Pepsi from the fridge. When I turned around, something caught my eye in the window. Nevin was walking across my backyard. I grabbed an extra can of Pepsi and headed outside. It was much quieter without the noise of the lawn mower.

Nevin's tan, muscular body glistened with sweat. His shoes were covered in grass clippings. He stood next to Hunter, sunglasses and baseball cap on. He gave me a partial smile. "Hey, Winter."

I handed Hunter a Pepsi, then held one out to Nevin. "Thirsty?"

"Definitely." He popped the top and guzzled it down. Hunter only took a sip of his.

Nevin glanced around the backyard. "You want me to bring the mower over and cut the grass? I could hit the front yard too while I'm at it."

There wasn't much grass to mow. Most of the yard was

covered by cement, gravel, or mulch. But I decided I would take him up on his offer since it wouldn't be too much work, and I didn't want to have to do it. "Okay. Thanks."

He smiled. "I'll send you a bill when I'm done."

Hunter cocked his head. "A bill?"

Nevin started laughing. "I was just kidding. Of course I'll do it for free. I'm on Hunter's dime right now."

I didn't want Hunter paying for this. "Don't worry about it, Nevin. The grass is fine. I don't need you to mow it."

Hunter shook his head. "He's already got the mower out anyway. It won't be a big deal for him to come over and mow your yard. I don't need him to do anything else for me right now."

I would be taking advantage of Hunter, and I didn't feel right about that. Nevin should have offered to mow my lawn when he was off the clock. "The lawn doesn't need to be mowed. Seriously, don't worry about it." I shot Nevin a look, irritated by his helpful and generous offer that wasn't really helpful or generous at all. He was a jerk.

"I didn't mean to make this complicated," Nevin said, his smile much smaller.

Yeah, well, you did, I wanted to say.

Hunter breathed out a heavy sigh as the corners of his mouth turned down.

Nevin guzzled down the rest of his Pepsi, then crushed the can in his hand. Was he trying to show off how strong he was? I wanted to tell him that I wasn't impressed.

"So what were you two talking about before I got here?" Nevin asked.

"I don't remember," I said, becoming more irritated by his intrusion. Didn't he have work to do?

Hunter took another drink. I wondered if Nevin's presence bothered him too. He wasn't paying him to hang out and visit.

There were a few beats of silence before Nevin spoke again. "Have you ridden the Ferris wheel down by the pier yet, Winter?"

"No, not yet."

"The three of us should go some time. Don't you think so, Hunter?"

"Yeah, that'd be fun." Hunter shifted in his chair, about to stand up. Max opened his eyes, springing to his feet. "It's getting way too hot out here. I'm gonna head in."

Nevin reached for Hunter's Pepsi. "You finished? I can take that."

"Yep. I'm done."

Nevin crushed Hunter's can too. I almost rolled my eyes. Show-off.

"So should we go to the Ferris wheel tonight?" Nevin asked. "How about it, Winter? Are you free?"

I did want to ride the Ferris wheel, but not with Nevin. "Can't tonight. I'm busy."

"See ya, Winter," Hunter said, holding on to Max's harness.

"See ya around," Nevin chimed in, following behind.

"Bye." I sat there watching them walk away, wondering if Nevin was going to make a habit of showing up over here. I sure hoped not.

CHAPTER 9

MILTON

When I turned fourteen, I discovered a new obsession—besides sharks. Her name was Holly. She was my very first girlfriend. My first kiss.

We were in two of the same classes. She lived down the street from me, so we also rode the same bus. I just knew we were meant to be together.

The first time I built up enough courage to talk to her was on that bus. Her best friend was absent that day, so the seat next to her was open. Before I approached, I ran my finger over the shark tooth in my pocket. "Can I sit there?" I asked, motioning to the seat next to her.

Holly had pale skin, so much so that I saw her cheeks turn red right in front of my eyes. I took that to mean that she was just as nervous as I was. "Yeah," she replied, her voice cracking. She cleared her throat. "Go ahead."

When I sat down, I felt my cheeks burn too, though I doubted she could tell. My skin wasn't nearly as pale as hers. "Did you know that we're practically neighbors? You live down the street from me."

Holly shook her head. "I didn't know that. Which house?"

Of course she didn't know. The bus always picked her up before me in the morning. "I live in the green house with the red truck." The red truck was always parked in the driveway, because it had something wrong with it and my dad had no idea how to fix it. "You should come over sometime," I said. Holly's cheeks turned red again.

The next day, her best friend was back on the bus again, only she wasn't sitting with Holly. She was sitting in the seat in front of her. That was how I knew that Holly liked me. Plus, she smiled really big when she saw me. So this time I didn't even ask. I just took the seat next to her like I belonged there.

Sitting next to each other on the bus became our routine. We even started eating lunch together at school. Then a couple weeks after that, Holly came over to my house while my parents were at work. I picked that day to invite her over because I knew that my brother would be at his part-time job.

We sat in the family room, watching a shark documentary. I only suggested watching it because Holly acted like she was interested in sharks. At least she seemed like she was when I showed her my shark tooth. I thought things went well. Holly seemed like she had a good time, at least I thought she did.

But the next day on the bus, her best friend was sitting right next to her, in my spot. Holly didn't even look at me when I said hi to her. At lunch, I couldn't find her anywhere. On the bus ride home from school, the same thing happened.

I didn't understand. I thought she liked me. What changed? When I finally got a chance to talk to her after class the next day at school, she couldn't get away from me fast enough. She barely said anything to me, giving some excuse about needing to hurry to her next class.

Since trying to talk to her at school or on the bus wasn't working, I had to get her someplace where we wouldn't be interrupted. So I followed her off the bus.

"Holly," I called, stopping at the edge of her driveway. "Can we talk?"

Her eyes got all wide. "What are you doing here?"

"I was just wondering if maybe you'd want to come over or something."

She shook her head rapidly, curls flying. "No." She hugged her purse into her chest. "I can't."

"Why not?"

Her eyes darted around looking everywhere but at me. "Because I'm busy." Holly spun around and practically ran to the front door. She slammed it shut, leaving me on the curb, like I meant nothing to her. But I knew that wasn't true. After all, we had kissed. Several times. That had to have meant something, didn't it?

I started walking home, feeling confused and totally

rejected. My brother noticed that I was acting differently. Normally I went straight to the kitchen after school to get something to eat, but that day I didn't feel hungry at all.

"What's the matter?" he asked, mocking me with a pouty face. "Are you all sad because your little girlfriend broke up with you?"

Holly hadn't broken up with me. Not exactly. Or maybe she did. "How do you know about that?"

My brother didn't ride the bus. He got a ride from one of his friends. And he had a different lunch period than us. I rarely saw him at school at all, so how did he even know about Holly and me?

The doorbell rang. "Right on time," he said with a grin.

When he opened the door, I couldn't believe my eyes. "Holly?" I jumped up from the couch, wondering if she had come to apologize and make up with me. I started toward the door, but stopped dead in my tracks. My brother had wrapped his arms around her, pulled her in and started kissing her right in front of me. And Holly was kissing him back.

I felt tears sting my eyes. How could my brother betray me like this? How could he stoop so low as to steal my girlfriend away from me?

Their kiss wasn't short. Like staring at a car crash, I didn't want to see it, but I couldn't look away. It seemed like it would never end. At least neither of them noticed the tears in my eyes. Once I gained enough composure to finally move my legs, I got out of there as fast as I could.

While Holly was still at our house, my brother sent me a text message. It was a picture of them kissing.

I asked him the next day how long he had been seeing Holly behind my back and he said, "That's not a very gentlemanly thing to ask, now is it?"

Gentlemanly? I wanted so badly to punch him in the face. But I knew he would kill me if I tried. There was nothing I could do to hurt him that came close to what he had done to me.

About two weeks later, my brother had moved on from Holly, but not until after he had sent me tons more pictures of them, all for the purpose of rubbing their relationship in my face.

I managed to get over Holly. Her best friend Jill helped with that. She agreed that what Holly and my brother had done was coldhearted and mean. She was sympathetic to my situation and wanted to help me feel better. I soon learned that helping me feel better meant that she wanted the two of us to be a couple.

Jill knew everything about what happened between my brother and Holly. I told her how he had once tried to kill me—burying me alive. How he would randomly attack me for no reason, and put duct tape over my mouth and nose until I passed out. I told her about how he held me under the water at the beach. Salt water went up my nose and down my throat. I barely survived.

After hearing all of this, I would have thought that Jill

would know better than to talk to him. She should have been furious with him. She should have hated him for what he had done to me. But no, Jill turned out to be just like Holly. The only difference between them was that Jill told me right to my face that she wanted to break up with me.

When my brother's new barrage of text messages predictably began arriving I felt like I couldn't breathe. It was almost as bad as when he tried to bury me alive in the sand. I was gasping and coughing like I couldn't catch my breath.

Mom told me later that I was having a panic attack. I heard her talking to my dad about how freaked out I was. It made him angry. He thought I was being weak. "No son of mine is gonna melt down like a crybaby." That's what he called me: a "crybaby."

Then Mom got all mad, not because she thought my dad was being cruel, but because she didn't want to have to deal with a son who had "emotional problems."

I felt so alone and broken. There was no one in my family I could turn to for support. When I tried to confide in a teacher at school, all she did was contact my parents. That only made things worse for me at home. My dad really gave it to me that night. But all my bruises were hidden by my shirt. I was his punching bag, literally. After he was done with me, my brother started in with a fresh round of taunts and insults.

"Are you going to go cry to your teacher again? Huh, crybaby?" Then he kicked me and said, "Since you're too stupid to figure this out for yourself, I'm going to lay it out for you. If Dad finds out you tattled on him a second time, he'll kill you."

That was the last time I allowed myself to cry. It was the last time I would let anyone know what I was feeling. I kept those things locked up deep inside.

After I turned fifteen, I found some confidence again and started pursuing another girl. When that first text message came from my brother with a picture of my girl cheating on me with him, all my emotions came boiling up. I spun out of control, completely destroying my bedroom, but I didn't cry. Not one tear.

A friend at school told me that my brother was stealing my girlfriends on purpose and bragging about it. He said, "It's no surprise that these girls go wild over your brother. He's totally out of their league. Of course they're jumping at the chance to be with him."

That made a lot of sense, because none of my girlfriends were out of *my* league. They weren't popular nor were they particularly pretty. They were like me—kind of plain.

With my fourth girlfriend, I tried to be more selective. I chose someone who was basically ugly and chubby. I genuinely thought I had found the right girl for me. I thought Susanna would see me as a catch, someone totally out of *her* league. That was my hope, anyway. I also warned her to stay away from my brother, told her that he was a player and would use her. Later that same night, I caught her cheating with him.

After that, I was way guarded. If a girl was friendly, or even just said "hi" to me, I questioned her motives. Yet at the same time, I still had a small sliver of hope. Surely there had to be at least one good girl among all the rotten ones who would genuinely be interested in me and not my brother, wasn't there?

In order to find her, I decided that I would go out with any girl who showed interest in me. That way I could test her loyalty right from the start and weed through all the bad ones. So I invited each girl over to my house while my brother was there, left them alone together and waited to see what happened… Not one of them passed the test.

This perpetual cycle of pain was becoming more than I could take. I was growing more cynical, even hostile, realizing that a good girl just simply didn't exist in the world. They were all the same: ruthless, manipulative, deceitful liars. Instead of allowing them to break me over and over again, I decided to start breaking them. They were going to feel my pain.

CHAPTER 10

WINTER

Our new renters had officially moved in: Tamara Gold and Tim Woods. Tamara was the same girl Mom and I had met the day we moved here—the girl with the breast implants and the nose job.

Before she moved in, Mom actually asked her if her breasts were real. I couldn't believe she just came right out and asked her that, but at the same time I was glad that she did. I wanted to see if Tamara would lie, figuring that if she did, this would be a huge sign that we shouldn't rent to her. To my surprise, Tamara told the truth. She admitted they were fake. I almost asked her about her nose next, but I wasn't as bold as Mom.

Tamara's lips definitely looked like they had been filled with collagen since the last time I had seen her. Maybe she really was addicted to plastic surgery.

Through the course of our interview with her, we learned that

Tamara didn't have any references, and she didn't have a job. When Mom asked her for proof of identification, she claimed her purse had been stolen and she hadn't replaced her driver's license yet. Then she pulled out a stack of cash from her purse and said, "Here's the deposit, plus six months' rent in advance."

When Mom saw all that money, her face just lit up. She asked, "When can you move in?"

Things got off to a good start. There hadn't been any problems with Tamara or Tim, other than Tamara getting on my nerves and Tim tracking mud through the house. Oh, and they were both slobs.

Mom told me I should be grateful, because now at least we had money coming in. I was grateful. She didn't need to remind me.

As I sat at the kitchen counter, I felt the warmth of the morning sun through the windows. I was enjoying the peace and quiet and the fruity flavor of my breakfast cereal when Tamara walked in wearing an impossibly tiny yellow bikini.

"Hey, kid," she said.

"My name's Winter," I replied with deliberate irritation. I had already told her my name several times before. I was eighteen, not a child, or a *kid*. She said she was twenty-two. I wondered if she was lying, because she didn't seem that old.

Tamara pulled out an empty jug from the fridge. "No way," she huffed. The refrigerator door slammed shut, glass containers rattling. "Who drank the last of my grapefruit juice?" She stared at me, brows knit together.

I went ahead and shot a dirty look right back at her. How could she accuse me of stealing her disgusting grapefruit juice?

"I wrote my name on here for a reason." Tamara pointed to the jug with her fake fingernail. "See?" She tapped it like she wanted to make sure I understood how the claiming of food worked, just in case I was a total idiot.

"I think everyone in this house knows how to read. Maybe you drank it all and just forgot."

"No, I didn't. This was halfway full yesterday." She rested her hand on her bony hip. "I had this same problem the last place I lived. Some people just don't know how to respect other people's property." She jammed the empty jug into the overflowing trash can.

I moved the cereal box over to block her from my view and continued eating, already wishing that she didn't live here, only it was too late. Mom had taken all of Tamara's rent money and bought herself a new car. We were stuck with Tamara for another six months, at least. Somehow I was going to have to endure her annoying presence.

The house finally quieted down when Tamara stepped out the back door and headed to the beach. I hoped she would stay out there for the rest of the day.

After I finished watching a few episodes of a British detective show, I took the trash out, then began washing the dishes.

I was scrubbing the last dirty glass when the back door slid wide open, letting in a waft of hot air. Tamara came prancing through the door. I expected her to shut it, but somebody else walked in right behind her, and my mouth dropped open. What was Eli doing here? Were they seeing each other? Please don't let that be true. Eli, please be single and repulsed by Tamara.

She strolled past me, still giggling about some private conversation they had shared on their way in. "We have a ton of ice, Eli." She opened and closed drawers and cupboards. "Hey, kid, where do we keep the ziplock baggies?"

I couldn't believe she just called me "kid" in front of Eli. A dirty look was about to emerge on my face. I forced a smile instead but was sure I didn't look happy, because the smile felt uncomfortable. "I think we must be out."

Tamara sighed heavily. I expected her to accuse me of taking the ziplock baggies, just like she had accused me of drinking her grapefruit juice. She was probably thinking this at least. Tamara gave me an equally forced smile, then turned to Eli. "I'll be right back. I think I have some upstairs in my bedroom." She breezed out of the kitchen, leaving us alone.

The water in the sink was still running. I had a glass in my hand, along with a dishrag. I wasn't sure if I should finish cleaning it or just set it down.

"Sorry about barging in on you like this," Eli said in his deep, velvety smooth voice.

"It's no problem." He could barge in on me any time he wanted.

"What's your name?"

"Winter."

He pointed at me. "You're the first Winter I've ever met."

"Yeah, I've never met anyone else with my name either." The water was getting hot and starting to burn my hand. I reached for the handle to pull it forward and the glass slipped out of my hand, landing with a crash. I looked down at all the tiny shards of broken glass glistening in the sink. Great.

"Do you need some help cleaning that up?"

A sharp sting pricked my finger. "Ouch!" I jerked my hand back as a stream of blood began rolling down my finger.

Eli grabbed a handful of paper towels and sailed over to me. He rinsed my finger under the water, then inspected carefully before pressing the paper towels gently against my cut. My pulse sped up as he held my hand in his. "It doesn't look deep enough to require stitches. Where do you keep your first aid kit?"

"I think there might be some Band-Aids in the top drawer over by the trash can."

I stood there watching him as he took care of my cut, removing the paper towels and dabbing off the excess blood. His dark brown curls were peppered with sand. He must have gone swimming in the ocean today. His hair still looked a little damp.

Eli's dark eyes suddenly flashed up; he had caught me staring at him. "How does that feel?" he asked.

If he only knew...

He raised his eyebrows. "Does it still hurt?"

I shook my head. "You're pretty good at this."

He chuckled, pulling the trash can over. Then he started picking up the broken pieces of glass from the sink. I helped.

I didn't know what was going on between him and Tamara. I worried that she was trying to seduce him or already had. Even if they were still in the friendship stage, I didn't think I could compete with Tamara. Eli would never choose me over her. She was absolutely gorgeous.

I regretted that I hadn't found the courage to talk to Eli sooner. I had passed up way too many opportunities, and now it was too late. Tamara had already swooped in like a seagull to snatch him away.

As we worked side by side, I noticed a slight smile emerge on Eli's face, and I was dying to know what he was thinking.

"I've been meaning to talk to you," he finally said.

I wondered whether that was a good thing. "About what?"

"About anything," he said, his eyes still focused on the pieces of glass. "I've seen you around, and I was curious. I wanted to meet you."

"Curious?" I repeated, wondering what that meant. Maybe it was a good thing that he was curious about me. Being curious was better than being uninterested. "Well, I was curious about you too."

Eli smiled, and his smile was captivating, alluring, infectious. "What is it that you wanted to know?" he asked.

My gaze lowered to his lips. I had wondered what it would be like to kiss him, but I wasn't going to be so bold as to admit that right now. "I wanted to know how you could put up with Jaxson. Don't you just want to strangle him sometimes?" I teased.

Eli looked at me from the corner of his eye, smiling wider. "What's that supposed to mean? Do you know Jaxson?"

"No. I've just observed some things," I said with a shrug.

Eli cocked his head in interest. "What kinds of things have you observed?"

"Let's see…" I paused for dramatic effect. "I saw him kick sand over his gum instead of picking it up like you had asked him to. I've seen him stare down at his phone or watch girls instead of doing his job. And he is super loud when he talks. Even if I didn't want to listen to him, I couldn't tune his voice out. It carries through the air. Should I continue, or is that enough?" I smiled.

He stared at me inquisitively. "I had no idea that you even noticed us. Why haven't you come over to say hi or introduce yourself?"

I couldn't tell him that I was too chicken. I had to think of another excuse. "Because you're up on the lifeguard tower working, saving lives, keeping the swimmers safe. I didn't want to interrupt."

He raised an eyebrow, staring at me, and my stomach fluttered. I hadn't had this much direct eye contact with a guy in a long time. "I would come down in a heartbeat to talk to *you*."

His comment rocked me back on my heels. Was he flirting

with me? "You could have introduced yourself to me too, you know," I countered. "What was your excuse?"

"Yeah," he nodded, "I guess you're right. I could have come and talked to you. But do me a favor."

"What?"

"Next time you're out on the beach, don't be a stranger. At least wave or something."

"The same goes for you too." Just then, I noticed something move behind me. Turning around, I saw Tamara standing there with a scowl on her face. Then her expression softened, only slightly.

"Sorry it took me so long." She flicked her ponytail off her shoulder, heading to the freezer.

"Not a problem," Eli replied, dragging the trash can back to its usual resting place.

Tamara quickly began filling the bag with ice. A few cubes fell onto the floor, but she didn't bother to pick them up. "Alrighty. One ice pack, ready to go." She handed it to Eli.

"What's the ice pack for?" I asked.

"Somebody twisted their ankle," Eli replied.

The back door slid open again, and Jaxson walked in. His bright blond hair matched his white teeth. He nudged Eli out of the way, surveying the room, love handles hanging down over the waistband of his shorts, jiggling as he walked. "I thought I'd come check on you, brah. I wanted to make sure Tamara hadn't taken advantage of you."

Tamara flipped her ponytail, rolling her eyes. "I'm not like you, Jaxson. I would never take advantage of anybody."

He snapped his head around, glaring at her. "Quit the innocent act. You aren't fooling anybody."

Eli stepped in front of Jaxson, shoving the bag of ice into his chest. "You were supposed to stay out at the beach and watch the swimmers."

"Hey, I'm not getting paid to do your job too. You said you'd be right back. That was like twenty minutes ago, brah. I warned you not to go with that sleazy girl."

Whoa! My jaw just hit the floor.

"Excuse me?" Tamara snapped.

"I'm just speaking the truth," Jaxson said, smugly.

Tamara crossed her arms, eyes on Jaxson. "You're just mad because I turned you down when you asked me out."

Did Jaxson ask her out? Was his ego really that big? How could he possibly think that he would have a chance with her?

A look of shock spread across Jaxson's face. "I never asked you out." He turned to Eli. "I told you she's trouble."

"Let's go—come on." Eli took Jaxson by the shoulders, pushing him out the door.

Jaxson continued to accuse Tamara of being a liar, only to be silenced by the door closing.

I stood there in the kitchen waiting for Tamara to explain what had happened with Jaxson, or maybe even complain about him, but she didn't. She sat down on the couch with a content expression on her face, her fingers skating across the screen of her phone.

It surprised me that she wasn't upset anymore. It was as if nothing had happened. Wow. How could she just let it all go like that? That's so strange. I would definitely still be upset. Anybody would. I didn't understand. Did she not have any feelings? Or was she just that arrogant?

Tamara held her phone out to take a selfie. She looked at the picture on the screen, adjusted her ponytail, and took another one.

"Hey," I said.

"Yeah?" she replied, barely looking up at me.

"You're not mad at Jaxson anymore?"

She rolled her eyes, shaking her head. "He's a loser. Not even worth my time." Then she got up and walked out of the family room without saying another word.

Jaxson definitely was a loser. But still, I didn't understand the workings of Tamara's mind. Was she just so confident in herself that she didn't care what other people thought of her? Was that it?

I looked out the window, my eyes squinting in the bright sunlight. From a distance, I could see Jaxson and Eli sitting atop the lifeguard tower, the vast ocean spread out in front of them.

My thoughts focused on Eli. I was impressed at how he handled the altercation between Tamara and Jaxson. He kept his cool and stayed in control, managing to stop the situation from escalating.

My mind soon began replaying our conversation. There were so many things that I liked about him: his smile, his personality, his maturity. I couldn't wait to talk to him again. I continued thinking about Eli as I finished cleaning the rest of the downstairs.

I was feeling a lot more optimistic about the prospect that he and Tamara were not together. If they had been, then Eli most definitely would have decked Jaxson for being so rude to her. He wouldn't have let that go. He would have defended her.

The only cleaning I had left to do was the laundry. I headed up to the second floor and started a load of towels. When I walked back into the hallway, I noticed that Aunt Emma's bedroom door was cracked open, and the light was on. The door should have been locked. I knew Mom wasn't in there. She was at school. Which meant there were only two other options: Tim or Tamara.

CHAPTER 11

WINTER

I checked the closet and the bathroom, but nobody was in there. I continued to inspect Aunt Emma's bedroom, looking for anything that might have been missing or out of place. But the problem was, I had only come in here a few times before. I wasn't sure if I would even notice if something was different or gone.

The dressers were cleared of any clutter. Two brown leather recliners sat facing a flat-screen TV mounted above the fireplace. The bed was made. There weren't any dirty clothes in the hamper or on the floor. The trash can was empty. It almost looked staged. No personal effects, no personality. If it weren't for the photograph sitting on the nightstand, I wouldn't have known that this room had ever been Aunt Emma's.

I picked up the picture to get a closer look. Aunt Emma

was sitting next to Reginald on a park bench with a lake in the background, surrounded by green grass and tall trees. Aunt Emma had the same oval face and sandy blond hair as Mom. My eyes were the same hazel green color as hers. She looked beautiful, just like I remembered.

She was much younger than Reginald. He looked old enough to be her father, and the years hadn't been kind to him. His skin was tan, weathered, and wrinkled. He was overweight, and he didn't have much hair. But Aunt Emma was smiling in the picture, and so was he. They appeared to be happy. I hoped they were.

My mind quickly returned to the matter at hand as I set the picture back down. Who had been snooping in here? Was it Tamara or Tim, and why?

When I walked back out into the hallway, I saw Tim standing at the top of the staircase. If he had been the one in Aunt Emma's room, would he be standing there making it so obvious? He didn't seem that dumb.

Tim removed the construction hat from his head. "Hey, Winter. Can you tell your mom that I made extra copies of the house key for her? I left them on the table in the family room."

"Sure." I nodded as I moved toward the stairs.

"Can you also tell her that I fixed the back gate?"

"Okay." I hadn't realized that the gate needed to be fixed. It seemed to be working just fine for me.

Tim started down the steps in front of me, giving me a

perfect view of the bald spot on top of his head. If I had scissors in my hand, I'd be so tempted to cut his mullet off right now. I wasn't sure if his haircut was coming back into style, but regardless, it didn't look good on him.

When Mom and I interviewed Tim, he presented us with a reference letter from his previous landlord and one from his boss. Mom asked him if he could afford to pay rent. He of course said that he could and presented a check on the spot for the deposit and first month. The next words out of Mom's mouth were, "Are you single?" and then she laughed like she was joking, but I knew she wasn't. She was into him, and she hadn't stopped flirting with him since he moved in. Whether Tim was interested in her, I had no idea. He seemed much more reserved than Mom's typical type, almost shy.

Had Tim been snooping around in Aunt Emma's room? I was unsure, but for some reason I couldn't let it go. I had to say something to him.

When we arrived at the bottom of the staircase, I said, "Tim. Did you go into the bedroom at the end of the hall?"

His eyes squinted as he considered my question. Then he shook his head. "The only bedrooms I've been in are mine and your mom's."

What? He's been in Mom's bedroom? Why? "My mom's?"

"Yeah, uh…" he hesitated. "She wanted me to fix a leaky faucet in her bathroom." He pointed over his shoulder. "I gotta go to work. I'm gonna be late."

I sure hoped it was just a leaky faucet. Mom didn't need the distraction of a relationship right now. She needed to focus on school. Plus, we needed a tenant who paid rent in cash, not a boyfriend who mooched off us.

I stopped at the front door, remembering that I had forgotten my purse upstairs. By the time I retrieved it and came outside, Tim's truck was already gone. The only vehicle left in the driveway was mine. Mom had given me the old SUV. I was grateful to have transportation, but it was ugly and didn't work that well, so it was more of a love-hate relationship.

Just before I stuck the key in the ignition, Tamara came running out of the house, waving her arms. "Hey, wait!"

My window was already rolled down, so I couldn't act like I didn't hear her, although I considered it. Tamara didn't own a car, so I suspected she wanted a ride somewhere.

She had told Mom and me that she preferred to hire an Uber driver or a taxi. She said that she had been in a bad accident, and ever since then she was afraid to drive. But I didn't believe her. Tamara oozed self-confidence all the time, no matter the situation. I didn't think anything or anyone scared her.

There had to be another reason that she didn't own a vehicle. It couldn't have been because of a lack of money, at least I didn't think so. But then again, she didn't have a job. Maybe she had already used up most of her money when she paid us all that rent in advance.

"Can you give me a ride to the store?"

"I've got someplace I need to go," I said, cranking the engine.

"I'll give you gas money, and I'll buy you lunch."

I sat there for a moment considering her offer. The gas money was tempting, and I *was* hungry. "Okay."

Tamara ran around to the passenger side, hopped in, and slammed the door shut. "Does the air conditioner not work?"

"It hasn't worked in years."

She sighed, rolling her eyes.

"Do you still want a ride?"

She sighed again. "I have to get something. It can't wait."

I backed the SUV out of the driveway. The engine sputtered until I hit the gas and took off down the street.

Tamara peeled off her shirt and was now only wearing a skimpy bikini top. "So where are you headed?"

"To the post office."

"Are you mailing a package?" She turned and looked in the back seat.

"No. I'm just picking up some of my aunt Emma's mail and closing her post office box account." Mr. Davis had given Mom and me the key. I had almost forgotten I needed to take care of this.

Tamara kicked off her flip-flops and propped her bare feet up onto the dash. "I might as well go in too. I need to buy some stamps."

What did she need to buy stamps for? She didn't seem like the type to write letters, unless she was writing to someone in prison. I smiled, wanting to laugh out loud at my own joke.

When we arrived at the post office, we headed inside and

Tamara started following me. I did not bring her here so she could be my shadow. We weren't friends, and this trip wasn't for the purpose of hanging out together. "Um," I paused, turning to look at her. "You can go ahead and get in line."

"I suppose you want me to save you a spot."

No, I wanted her to stay out of my business.

She spun around and walked off, flip-flops smacking against her feet.

Aunt Emma's mailbox was crammed full of junk mail. I stuffed it all into my purse and somehow it magically fit.

Tamara motioned for me to get in line with her. "Why did your aunt have a post office box? Seems kind of strange since there's a mailbox right in front of your house."

I shrugged in response. Honestly I didn't know why. I thought it was strange too.

"Why didn't you and your mom live with your aunt? She had plenty of room."

This was none of her business. I wished that Mom had never told Tamara and Tim that we inherited Aunt Emma's house. Our renters didn't need to know about our private lives.

"You sure ask a lot of questions."

"I do?" she replied, sounding surprised. "I'm just trying to get to know you better."

Why would she want to do that? I doubted she wanted to be friends with me, and I didn't want to be friends with her either.

After we left the post office, we made a quick trip to the grocery store, then started toward home. Tamara took off her seat belt and leaned over the seat. Plastic bags rattled. I glanced up and looked in the rearview mirror as she rummaged through her grocery sacks. My eyes returned to the road. This girl was so distracting and annoying.

When I looked in the mirror again, I saw her reach inside my purse. "What are you doing?"

"What?" she replied, still rummaging through it, as if she wasn't doing anything wrong.

The car next to me laid on its horn. I swerved back into my lane, barely missing it.

"Whoa!" Tamara flipped back around and braced herself against the dash.

I slowed down, trying to refocus on the road. "What were you doing in my purse?"

"I was just looking for some coupons in your aunt's junk mail." She held up a sheet of fast-food coupons. "This place is just a couple miles from here. Buy two burgers and get two fries free."

"Tamara!" I snapped.

"What?"

"Don't ever go through my purse again! We may live in the same house, but that doesn't mean that you can go through my things."

"Okay, fine," she mumbled, then said something under her breath about her grapefruit juice.

When we arrived at home, I went straight up to my bedroom so I could eat by myself. I was still mad at her for going through my purse.

I sat on my bed with my hamburger and fries, and started sifting through Aunt Emma's mail, which was mostly all junk. I picked up a stack of advertisements and walked over to the trash can. A small envelope slipped out and landed on the floor. Aunt Emma's name and address was scrawled on the front of it. There was no return address. I ripped it open, pulled out a folded piece of white paper, and began reading:

> Emma,
> This is your final warning! Like I told you before, you have until midnight, Friday, to bury the item under the lifeguard tower behind your house. If you fail to do this, you'll be sorry!

Who wrote this? What did they mean by "you'll be sorry"? This note wasn't exactly a death threat, but it was pretty close. My mind continued to hover over this chilling new revelation. Maybe Aunt Emma's fall hadn't been an accident. Maybe somebody pushed her down the stairs and killed her on purpose.

I picked up the envelope, just now realizing that it didn't have a stamp. This letter hadn't been mailed to her. Someone must have slipped it inside her post office box.

According to the letter, this wasn't the first one she had

received. I wondered where the other letters were. Had she called the police? Mr. Davis didn't mention anything about this. He never implied that her death could have been anything other than an accident. He showed Mom and me the police report. There was no mention of any suspicion of foul play or any investigation.

My heart sank, knowing it would be almost impossible to prove that Aunt Emma had been murdered. It was Mom's idea to get her cremated. I knew I didn't feel good about that for some reason. I wished I would have said something to Mom, but I didn't, and now it was too late.

CHAPTER 12

MILTON

Most of my problems went away when I started living the life of a con man. I had finally accepted the truth: I couldn't beat my brother at his game. No matter how hard I tried, girls would keep dumping me for him. They would smile at me, lie to my face, and leave the second he gave them attention. It didn't matter what I said or did. They always betrayed me.

So I stopped playing by their rules—and his. I started my own game. A game where I was in control. I decided I would manipulate girls the way they had manipulated me. Use them the way they used me.

At first, I wasn't sure I could pull it off. I didn't think I had it in me. But once I got started, I found out it wasn't that hard. And with a little practice, I got good. Really good.

I learned something early on: When a girl thinks the guy

she's dating can't see her imperfections, she lets her guard down. She flirts more, trusts faster, drops her insecurities. She assumes she's safe.

I went by the name Milton Thorne, used a cane, and wore dark sunglasses. Pretending to be blind didn't just get me sympathy. It got me attention. It got me dates. And more than that, it made me money.

Women had no idea that I was watching them when they typed their passwords and PIN numbers. I had access to jewelry, cash, credit cards, and anything else of value lying around. They didn't think twice about leaving me alone in their homes, trusting I couldn't see the jewelry box on the dresser or the cash-stuffed jar in the kitchen cupboard. They trusted me, and they shouldn't have.

When I was growing up, my parents never thought that I would amount to much. They said I was too stupid to go to college, because I didn't get good enough grades.

When I was a sophomore in high school, my brother snatched my report card out of my hand and stuck it to the front of the fridge with a magnet, right next to his.

"Mom and Dad are gonna flip when they see this," he grinned. "Especially Dad."

I didn't get any F's but there were plenty of C's and D's. My brother's lowest grade was a B.

"Give it back," I said, lunging for it, but he blocked me, pushing me back so hard I almost fell. I had planned on altering my report card to avoid getting in trouble. With one careful stroke of a pen I could change those D's to B's. Time was running out. I let out a loud yell, full of frustration and anger, almost animallike.

My brother started laughing, mockingly. "You are a freak, you know that?"

I hated him so much. There was no doubt in my mind that he wouldn't stop until Dad got home. The only option I had left was to try and negotiate with him. "What do you want?" I asked. "What can I do to make you give it back?"

My brother thought about it for a minute, then a sly smile spread across his face. "Give me your shark tooth."

"What?" I said, totally taken aback. I thought he had forgotten about my lucky shark tooth. He hadn't tried to steal it from me in years. "No," I said, firmly. "I'm not giving that to you."

He shrugged. "Then I'm not giving you your report card back."

"I'll do anything else. Anything. Just please give that back to me."

My brother considered this for a bit, the wheels in his head turning. I swallowed hard, hoping he would come up with another option.

"Okay. If I give you your report card back, then you owe me three favors." He pointed at me, one eye narrowed. "You have to do whatever I want, whenever I say. And if you don't, then I'll make you pay."

I knew he meant it. He always did. If I crossed him, he

would get his revenge. I considered his proposal, wondering what those favors might possibly be. I felt like I was selling my soul to the devil, but I agreed to do it anyway.

When it came time for the favors to be collected, I was not prepared for the level of risk involved.

The first favor was for me to steal Dad's credit card from his wallet. I waited until Dad was asleep, then snuck into my parents' bedroom and grabbed it. My brother used the credit card to buy some things online, but I didn't know what.

The second favor was more intense. My brother had made an arrangement to meet up with someone who was selling their gaming system. My job was to wear a mask and run up and snatch it before any money was exchanged. This way my brother would get the gaming system for free. I thought for sure I would get caught, or something would go wrong, but somehow we got away with it.

The last favor was a big one. Again, my brother had me wear a mask. It was dark out and we were in the school parking lot. This girl he liked, a cheerleader, had just returned from a basketball game at some other school. The bus pulled into the parking lot, dropping off all the cheerleaders.

I waited in the shadows, ducked behind a car, until I saw her walk by. Then I grabbed her from behind, my hand over her mouth. My brother had me practice this particular move with him over and over again until I got it right, so I knew exactly how to do it. The girl was petite, easy to control. I held her there while she struggled to get free, giving my brother a chance to come to her rescue and be the hero.

The part we didn't practice was him punching me in the face so hard I saw stars. Feeling dazed and barely able to maintain my balance, I somehow managed to escape before more people came, drawn by the girl's screams.

These three favors I did for my brother stuck with me. Each time, I had been totally full of fear, afraid I might get caught. But then, afterward, I was left with this unexpected feeling of euphoria. The rush was addictive. I started craving it and feeling confident in the idea that I could repeat those same kinds of things on my own. I knew I could do it. The only thing left was to make a plan of my own and execute it.

No one guessed that I was lying about being blind. After all, who would dare do something as despicable as that? I would. I didn't have a problem with it. I was just giving these females exactly what they deserved. Pretending to be blind was the ultimate con. But the more I did it, the more I realized that money wasn't the only thing I wanted. I started craving control. Dominance. Power.

CHAPTER 13

WINTER

I wondered if Aunt Emma actually did what that letter instructed her to do. Were the threats leveled at her so ominous that she felt compelled to comply? Still, I had a hard time imagining her sneaking out onto the beach in the dead of night to bury some mystery object underneath the lifeguard tower.

After reading the letter, I spent a solid ten minutes resisting the urge to go out onto the beach and start digging. But by the eleventh minute, curiosity got the best of me, and I changed my mind. I kept wondering, *what if?* What if the item she buried was still there? Or what if there was another letter buried there?

I stepped out onto the balcony to survey the beach. There were people everywhere and brightly colored umbrellas to provide them with shade; swimmers congregated in the surf.

The sun was shining, not a cloud in the sky. I could see the back of Eli's head as he sat atop the lifeguard tower next to Jaxson.

Over the next couple of hours, I kept watch out the back window from downstairs in the family room, waiting for Eli and Jaxson to leave. I turned on the TV and flipped through the channels, stopping at a crime documentary, wondering if one day Aunt Emma's story would be told on such a show.

While I couldn't prove she had been murdered, I felt like this was the only explanation that made sense. Her death being ruled as accidental never sat well with me before, kind of like a pebble in my shoe. I felt like something wasn't quite right, but I couldn't put my finger on it. I had chalked it up to guilt over the lack of contact I'd had with Aunt Emma and how I felt so disconnected from her, when all along it had been something more, something much worse. Now I felt like the fog had finally lifted from my mind, and I could see everything clearly. Aunt Emma couldn't have died from accidentally falling down the stairs. Somebody murdered her.

The back door slid open and Tamara came in. She picked up her phone that had been charging in the living room. When she finished checking it, she stood in front of the mirror that hung above the fireplace, staring at her reflection. She adjusted her ponytail, then moved around the couch to sit down on the coffee table directly in front of me. "I wanted to apologize about that whole digging-through-your-purse-thing. I swear, I wasn't trying to steal money from you or snoop around in your private things. I saw the coupons sticking out and was really craving a burger. I'm not really a coupon person. I just figured, why not? The coupon was right there, so I might as well use it…"

As she continued to apologize, a new realization hit me and I could no longer pay attention to what she was saying. I hadn't thought of this until just now, but it was obvious. I should have made the connection before. Was Tamara really just interested in coupons, or was she trying to steal the letter? Had she written it, or did she know who did? Was she connected to the murderer somehow?

"Winter," she said, waving her hand in front of my face, ripping me from my thoughts. "So are we good now? Because I don't want to have any tension between us, especially since we live under the same roof." She tilted her head, looking at me all innocent-like with her doe eyes. What an act.

Why was she so determined that I forgive her right at this moment? Did she think it could really be that simple? I did not trust her. Her apologies were worthless to me. "Just don't do it again," I said, still trying to process who she was and what she was up to.

"Did you not hear me?" she asked, looking at me like I was stupid. "I already said that I wouldn't do it again."

Yeah, because the letter wasn't in my purse anymore. I had it in my pocket, out of reach. Why did she want to live here? Was it for the purpose of getting the letter? Was there something else she was after? She must have been the one who went through Aunt Emma's bedroom. It wasn't Tim who did it.

"Tamara," I said, still getting used to the idea that I might be looking into the eyes of a murderer. "Stay out of the bedrooms in this house that aren't yours."

She shot me a questioning look as if she was totally caught off guard. "What are you talking about?"

"Someone was in my aunt's bedroom earlier today. That room is off-limits—nobody is allowed in there. That's why we lock the door."

"Trust me, Winter. I have no interest whatsoever in snooping through bedrooms, purses, or anything else that doesn't belong to me. Do you believe me?"

I wanted to tell her no. "Time will tell," I replied.

"Well, until you do feel like you can believe me, I would appreciate it if you'd just give me the benefit of the doubt and stop accusing me of things that you have no proof of. I fully accept the purse thing. But I did not go into your aunt's room."

"Same goes for me. I'd appreciate the benefit of the doubt as well," I said, sitting forward and staring at her, trying to act like I wasn't intimidated or afraid, even though I was.

She blinked in surprise. "Do you think I accused you of something?"

I cocked my head, trying to find some confidence. "I didn't drink your grapefruit juice."

Tamara smiled. "That was more of a PMS thing. I wasn't

accusing you of drinking my grapefruit juice." She shook her head, ponytail flying. "I'm sure it was Tim who drank it. He's like a human garbage disposal, eating and drinking everything he can get his hands on. I was just venting. Now I know that you're real sensitive, so I'll be more cautious with the kinds of things I say." She smiled at me again, but her eyes weren't smiling. And I was no longer intimidated. I was furious.

She called me *sensitive*?

Talking to her was exhausting. I felt like she was deliberately trying to mess with my head, like she was telling me that the sky was green when it clearly was blue. She had accused me of drinking her grapefruit juice, once in the kitchen, and a second time in the car after I yelled at her for digging through my purse.

"I'm glad we had this little talk," she said, smiling at me again like she was a therapist and I was her patient.

I heard the front door open as Tamara walked out of the room, and my eyes flicked over to the clock on the wall. It was barely past five. Mom was home early. I pulled the letter out of my pocket.

Mom walked right past me, straight to the kitchen cupboard. "I have a terrible headache," she moaned. "I need some Excedrin."

"Mom, I've got to show you something." I held out the folded piece of paper and explained how I had found it.

Mom pinched the bridge of her nose, eyes shut. She leaned

back against the counter. "Winter, I can't read this right now. Just tell me what it says."

After I read the letter, she opened her eyes and took the piece of paper from me. She read it over quickly, then handed it back.

"So, what do you think?" I asked. "Should we call the police?"

"And tell them what?" Mom picked up her glass of water and took another drink.

"That somebody might have pushed Aunt Emma down the stairs, and this letter is proof. Her death might not have been an accident."

Mom sighed, rubbing her forehead. "I'm no detective, but I've seen enough *CSI* episodes to know that this letter doesn't prove anything." Mom dumped the rest of her water into the sink.

"Someone was threatening her."

"Yeah, well, that's a huge leap to take. One stupid little note doesn't mean she was murdered. Need I remind you that Emma liked to drink? A lot?" The tone in Mom's voice changed. I could hear the hatred she had for Aunt Emma, and I could see it on her face. "She was probably drunk when she fell down those stairs." Mom shook her head. "You shouldn't feel sorry for her."

"She...died," I said, feeling defeated. Disappointed.

"Yeah. And so did Kyle." Mom's eyes suddenly turned red, filling with tears.

I couldn't believe she mentioned his name. She hadn't done that in years.

Mom took a deep breath, closing her eyes. I stood there, staring at her, wondering if she was going to say anything else about Kyle.

Sometimes I wondered if it wasn't Aunt Emma who Mom was really mad at. I wondered if she was mad at herself, or maybe me. Did she feel responsible for Kyle's death? Had Aunt Emma's accusation made her feel guilty? Lots of parents let their infants cry in the crib at night. Mom hadn't done anything wrong. And the same was true for Aunt Emma. Lots of people put babies to sleep on their stomachs. It wasn't Aunt Emma's fault that Kyle died, and it wasn't Mom's either. He died of sudden infant death syndrome.

Before Kyle was born, I made him a blanket. I had used some of Aunt Emma's sewing supplies and scraps of fabric. I had watched a YouTube video and learned how to sew the fabric together. I was only ten, but I had done a decent job. Mom loved it so much that she laid the blanket over the mattress in the crib, tucking it for him to lie on. He died on that blanket. I had heard Mom and Aunt Emma talking about the satin fabric, how it had smothered him.

Mom rubbed her forehead, letting out a heavy sigh. "I just want to go to bed and sleep this headache off." She grabbed a box of crackers and a bottle of water before disappearing down the hall. She hadn't even noticed the tears in my eyes.

I had already cried thousands of times over the loss of Kyle.

I didn't want to cry again, but Mom had mentioned his name, and it felt like an old wound had just been ripped back open. Plus, I was upset about Aunt Emma, knowing that someone cut her life short. She didn't deserve to die either. There wasn't anything I could do to bring either of them back. But I could bring the murderer who killed Aunt Emma to justice. I was already getting close. I just needed to figure out a way to prove that Tamara killed her or was somehow involved.

I wiped a tear from my eye and poured myself a glass of water, trying to regain my composure. As I was drinking it, I gazed out the window and almost choked. Jaxson and Eli were gone! This was the perfect time to dig. I would soon find out if there was another letter, or if the mystery item was still buried under the tower.

Before I took off for the beach, I stuck the letter inside one of the books on the bookshelf in the family room for safekeeping. I had never seen Tamara read a book, so I doubted she would find the letter.

When I arrived at the lifeguard tower, it dawned on me that I didn't have anything to dig with. Luckily there was a little girl nearby with an extra toy shovel. She let me borrow it.

From underneath the shade of the lifeguard tower, I dropped down to my knees and began scooping up the sand.

"Winter," a deep voice called, and my pulse rate spiked.

I looked up and saw Eli standing there. How was I going to explain what I was doing? I rose to my feet and brushed the sand off my knees. "Hi," I said, in an attempt to act casual.

His eyes darted to the toy shovel, then back to me again. "Are you building a sandcastle?"

He thought I was building a sandcastle? I guessed that was what this looked like. Sure. Of course it did. "Sorry, I thought you were gone."

He picked up the toy shovel and handed it to me. "I've still got another hour left on my shift."

Jaxson walked up behind Eli, staring at me inquisitively. "Do I know you? I think I've seen you somewhere before."

Was he being serious? Of course he has seen me. "You came into my house. I was in the kitchen."

Eli motioned to me. "This is Winter. She lives in Reginald Fontaine's old house."

What? I didn't know that Eli and Jaxson knew Reginald. Did they know Aunt Emma too?

Jaxson pointed at me, narrowing one eye. "You're the one who rents a room to Tamara. You should charge her double just for having to put up with her." He crossed his arms over his chest. "Why haven't I seen you go out in the ocean for a swim?"

"I'm not that great of a swimmer."

Jaxson looked down at my arms, my legs, then back to my eyes. "I could teach you."

There was no way I wanted him to give me swimming lessons.

"Sure you could," Eli teased, but Jaxson kept his eyes locked on to mine, waiting for me to answer.

I gazed out at the powerful waves crashing, one after another. There was nothing inviting about that sight. "What about the sharks?"

Jaxson barked out a loud laugh. "You're not really afraid of sharks, are you?"

Eli peeled his eyes away from the ocean, briefly, to look at me. "A shark has never attacked someone while I was on lifeguard duty."

How could Eli say that? Did he think I didn't know? "What about that girl who died?" I pointed in the direction where the unforgettable tragedy had occurred.

Eli palmed his curly hair back, moving it out of his eyes. "That happened somewhere else. It was the ocean current that washed her body to shore here. And we still don't know what happened to her. It might not have been a shark that killed her."

Jaxson nodded in agreement. "That girl had been dead for a while. Her body was stiff as a board, and pale—"

"I think she gets the picture," Eli cut him off.

Jaxson gestured to the right and then left, like he was a flight attendant pointing out emergency exits. "This here is a *no shark* zone. As long as you stay within this coned-off area, you'll be protected by me, so you don't have to worry. I'm also the best swimming instructor around. I can teach you how to avoid getting knocked over by the waves, what to do when there's a rip current, you name it. I can even teach you how to surf."

"No thanks." I shook my head, hoping he wouldn't continue to hound me about this.

"What?" Jaxson feigned offense, scratching his flabby belly. "Don't you trust me?"

Eli clapped his hand on Jaxson's shoulder. "Hey, if I don't trust you, then she definitely shouldn't trust you."

Jaxson pushed Eli's hand away and stepped in closer to me, crossing the invisible boundary line that marked my personal space. He stared at me with his pale blue—or were they green?—eyes.

"Who do you think is a better lifeguard?" Jaxson asked, pointing over his shoulder. "Me or him?"

What kind of a question was that? Did he really want to know the answer? Was he going to throw a fit and call me names when I told him what I thought? I guessed I was about to find out. "Eli has barely taken his eyes off the water this whole time we've been talking, while you, on the other hand, haven't looked out there at all."

Jaxson flashed me a big smile. His gaze focused on my lips. "I can't help it if I'm having a hard time keeping my eyes off you. You're distracting me."

That was not the reaction I expected. Maybe I would prefer him calling me names. "Then I guess I better leave, so I don't distract you anymore," I replied as I turned to walk away.

"See you around, Winter," Eli called.

"Bye," I replied.

After I returned the toy shovel to the little girl, I got the sense that somebody was watching me. I turned my head, my eyes sweeping across the beachgoers sprawled out along the shore, and suddenly my heart jolted. My entire body froze. I didn't know why I had a physical reaction like that when I saw who was looking at me. It was only Nevin.

He rose from his chair. His baseball cap and sunglasses were on, like usual, and his muscular body glistened in the sunlight due to a generous application of suntan oil. He walked toward me with a partial smile on his face, again careful not to show too many of his crooked teeth.

I heard somebody clear their throat, loudly, and I glanced back. It was Jaxson. He was standing about twenty feet away from me, next to a knocked-over caution cone. They had been set out to keep the area around the lifeguard tower clear of people. Jaxson's eyes remained on me, even when he bent down to pick up the caution cone. I glanced up at Eli sitting on top of the tower. His attention was on the ocean.

"Want to join me for a swim?" Nevin asked, drawing my attention.

A swim? "No thanks."

"Afraid of sharks?"

"I'm heading back to my house."

"So you're not afraid of sharks?"

Why was he pressing me on this? "I'd have to be a fool not to be a little concerned about running into a shark out there."

"Right." He nodded in agreement. "Especially after what happened to that girl... What was her name? I think it started with a P...Pamela, Penelope, or maybe it was Patrice." He snapped his finger. "Yeah, her name was Patrice."

I didn't remember hearing what the girl's name was.

"And then there was that other girl from last night," Nevin said, shaking his head.

"Last night?"

"Didn't you hear the news? Another dead girl was found. Not far from here." He gestured in the direction behind me down the beach. "Eyewitnesses reported that the girl looked like she had been killed by a shark."

I swallowed hard. Two shark attacks?

Nevin pointed to the lifeguard tower. "Jaxson was interviewed on the news. He said it looked like a shark got ahold of her. He was one of the people who helped pull her body out of the water. They interviewed some other witnesses too, and every one of them said the same thing. It was a shark attack." Nevin paused, shaking his head. "For some strange reason, the authorities aren't reporting on an official cause of death. Just like with that other girl, remember?"

Of course I remembered. It was impossible to forget. Mom and I had just moved here and hadn't even finished touring the house when we saw the commotion on the beach.

Nevin pulled out his phone, then swiped his finger across the screen. "Someone took a video of the girl being pulled out of the water and posted it on YouTube. You can see the teeth marks." He turned his phone to show me.

I averted my gaze, turning away. "I'll take your word for it."

He retracted his hand. "Too gory?"

"I'll watch it later." I wanted to watch it on my own, just in case it was too gory, so I could either stop it or skip ahead if I needed to.

Nevin slid his phone back into his pocket. "I've watched it like fifty times. That stuff doesn't bother me."

"Fifty? Why so many times?" Was he some kind of sicko?

"I thought I knew the girl, so I was trying to get a better look at her face." He shrugged. "But I couldn't tell if it was her."

"Well, hopefully it wasn't."

"Yeah, no kidding." He shrugged again, then gestured toward the ocean. "Look at all those people hanging out close to shore. They're afraid to go into the deep water. And I don't blame 'em, two shark attacks, so close together, and right around this area," he said, circling his finger as if drawing a line around the stretch of beach we were standing on.

"So you're not concerned about getting attacked by a shark?" I asked, wondering why he invited me to go for a swim.

"I like surfing way too much to give it up. Being around sharks, that's part of the thrill of it." He nodded toward the ocean. "But I was just going to take a quick dip before heading home. If you were to come along with me, I would have kept an eye out for the shark and protected you."

He couldn't possibly protect me from a shark. I knew he was just trying to act like a tough guy, and I wasn't impressed. "Well, be careful out there," I said, not really interested in continuing this conversation.

"I will." He headed back over to his chair, took off his hat and sunglasses, set his phone down, then jogged off toward the ocean.

As I walked away, I kept watch, wondering if he was really going for a swim.

He ran straight through the waves, then dove in. I wouldn't be caught dead doing something stupid like that.

Some people think that they're invincible, that nothing bad could ever happen to them. But my life experiences had taught me that wasn't true. Tragedy could strike at any moment, to anyone.

When I got back to the house, I tried searching for the YouTube videos Nevin was talking about, but I couldn't find them. I searched for the news report next, and I was able to find the one about the girl from last night. Yep, they did interview Jaxson and other eyewitnesses, just like Nevin had said.

I sat on the couch in front of the TV, my thoughts turning to the letter again. I wished I could have finished digging under the lifeguard tower. But maybe it wasn't a good idea to do that in broad daylight with so many people around. If by chance Tamara didn't write the letter, then there was someone else out there who did. Whoever that person was, I didn't want them finding out that I had read it.

I decided that I had better wait to go out there and dig until after it got dark, so nobody would see what I was doing.

CHAPTER 14

MILTON

Kendra looped her arm through mine as we walked into the club, guiding me toward the bar. "I hope you're ready to dance tonight, Milton!" I liked taking women to the club. Pretending to be blind gave me all kinds of possibilities on the dance floor. She leaned in close to my ear. "Because I'm ready." Kendra's perfume was sweet, but a little too strong. Typical. As soon as she realized she couldn't attract me with her looks, she started trying too hard with her scent.

I smiled the way she expected me to, letting her believe this night was about fun, romance, connection—whatever fantasy she was telling herself. Each date was getting me closer to her absolute unguarded trust. Soon, her bank account would be drained without a shred of suspicion pointed at me.

We found a table near the back, away from most of the noise. She ordered drinks for both of us, chatting the whole time like this was the perfect date. And for a moment, I almost let myself enjoy that make-believe. Almost.

Kendra and I had gone out three times before that night. Things had been going fine, or at least it seemed like they were. She laughed at my jokes. Held my hand. Said she didn't mind that I was blind. She liked how I didn't treat her like a trophy. Ha. She actually called herself a trophy. I almost laughed out loud at that. She was a four at best.

We were sitting at our table when her eyes suddenly lit up. "Oh, hi," she said, sounding way too excited when some guy appeared.

I kept my head facing forward, acting like I didn't notice. But through my sunglasses, I was watching everything.

"Hey," he said, leaning in to hug her. She didn't pull away.

Kendra's smile widened, dimples deepened. "What are you doing here?" she asked, all breathy.

"Well, you know, just hanging out. What about you? How've you been? It's been a long time."

She rested a hand on his arm like I wasn't even sitting next to her. "Pull up a chair and join us."

The guy barely glanced at me to acknowledge my presence. He snatched a chair from a nearby table, placing it right next to Kendra's.

I cleared my throat. "Kendra, who's your friend?" I asked, prompting her to introduce us.

"This is Mark. He's an old friend." She turned to him again. "How long has it been?"

He shrugged. "I don't know. Maybe six years."

"Six years," I repeated, unimpressed. "So where do you two know each other from?"

Kendra wrapped her arm around his. "He was my high school sweetheart."

The two of them sat there laughing and touching each other like I was invisible. He would whisper something in her ear, and she would throw her head back like it was the funniest thing she had ever heard. She touched his shoulder. He stroked her hand. I sat there, quiet, every second fueling my rage. They thought I couldn't see any of it. But I could. I saw everything.

Without warning, they stood up—arm in arm—and disappeared into the crowd.

No goodbye. No excuse. She just ditched me. Left me sitting there like I didn't matter.

On the outside I remained perfectly still as something deep inside began churning. The pain of the countless rejections I had suffered—a lifetime of injustices and humiliations—all came crashing together, filling me with an unquenchable fire.

Girls like Kendra always assumed they could get away with it. That I wouldn't notice. That there wouldn't be consequences. But there are always consequences. This wasn't about the money anymore. It was about respect. She owed me that. She owed me decency. She owed me for all the attention I had given her, the dates, the way I listened to her stupid ramblings and nodded like I cared.

Whatever happened next wasn't going to be my fault. It was on her. When you mess with a shark, you're gonna get bit. Kendra should have known that her day of reckoning would come, just like Patrice.

CHAPTER 15

WINTER

The house was quiet, except for the sound of the TV. Mom still hadn't come back downstairs. She was probably in bed trying to sleep off her headache.

Dirty dishes weren't piled up in the sink yet, which meant that Tim probably hadn't come home from work.

I assumed Tamara was in her bedroom. I hadn't seen her out on the beach. Those were the two likely places she would be, at least until nightfall. Then she would go out.

I hated not knowing Tamara's secrets. Was she a killer, or was she just a self-centered person incapable of harming anyone? Without knowing the answers to these questions, I doubted I would ever be able to relax in my own house again. I probably wouldn't get a good night's sleep either.

Night hadn't fallen yet, but it was getting close. I was still planning on going out after dark to dig, and this time I knew

I would need to bring my own shovel. As I searched through the garage, I came across an old red lunch box which sparked a memory from my childhood. When I was in second grade, Aunt Emma used to pack my lunch in a lunch box similar to this one. Then she would walk with me to the bus stop in the mornings, since Mom would be sleeping in after a night shift. That was one of my favorite memories of Aunt Emma.

I set the lunch box down and continued to scan the garage, until I spotted a shovel in the corner. Right next to it, sitting on a stack of boxes, I found a lantern and a head-mounted flashlight. Did Aunt Emma use these things when she buried the mystery item under the lifeguard tower? I was beginning to believe that my search tonight would actually uncover something.

Back inside the house, I began to feel increasingly anxious about the task ahead. I sat on the couch and watched some random TV show, just to pass the time.

Tamara walked into the family room wearing a fitted black-and-white-striped dress. This was the first time I had seen her wear something that actually covered most of her body.

She flicked her long blond hair off her shoulder. "So, how do I look?" She turned around, and I realized that her dress wasn't modest after all. It was backless.

"You look pretty," I replied. And she did. She always looked pretty—fake, but pretty.

"It's ladies' night until ten, so I'll be getting in for free."

She held up her hand, inspecting her fake nails, now painted bright pink. "Maybe I'll meet some hot, rich guy tonight."

"How do you know if a guy's rich?"

She shrugged. "Just the typical stuff; how many drinks he buys me, what kind of car he drives, how nice his house is… If he asks to go back to my place, that's a sure sign that he's broke and probably still lives with his momma, or he mooches off his friends."

"Or he's married," I added.

Tamara shrugged at my comment as if it didn't bother her, which wasn't surprising. A murderer wouldn't have any morals.

She unzipped her designer purse and started rummaging through it, the diamond bracelet on her wrist sparkling in the light from the TV. I wondered how she could afford such expensive things. How could she afford cosmetic surgery? How could she pay six months' rent in advance when she didn't have a job?

If she was rich, then why didn't she live in her own house or apartment?

Where did she get her money from?

I thought back to our trip to the store and our drive home when she was digging around in my purse, and then it occurred to me that maybe someone had paid her to get rid of the letter. Was that the type of work she did: dirty, underhanded, illegal things like that? Was that how she made her money?

Tamara sighed in annoyance, staring at her phone. "This old geezer is texting me, trying to ask me out." Her fingers skated across the screen. "I don't think so." She set her phone down, rolling her eyes. "Younger girls going out with older guys, that's so disgusting, don't you agree—oh, I forgot," she said, not sounding surprised at all. "Your aunt was going to marry that old guy."

How did she know about that? The only way I found out was by looking at the picture in Aunt Emma's bedroom. "Did you know Reginald and my aunt Emma?"

Tamara pulled out a tube of lip gloss from her purse and unscrewed the lid. She traced the pink lip gloss across her lips. "No. Your mom mentioned it to me." She rubbed her collagen-injected lips together, blending the gloss in. Her phone beeped. "My ride's here." She breezed out of the room.

I looked over at the shovel lying propped up against the wall, then my eyes shifted to the window and the hair on the back of my neck stood up. I couldn't see the moon or the stars. The sky was pitch black. It wasn't exactly the best night to go out there.

CHAPTER 16

MILTON

Throughout the day, I found myself dwelling on what happened to Kendra. I was wondering if I could make any improvements for the next time.

Eyewitnesses had reported that Kendra's injuries were consistent with a shark attack. Yet an official statement by the authorities hadn't been made, which angered me. I thought her injuries made it abundantly clear.

Maybe I needed to make some adjustments to my equipment. Maybe I needed to leave a few shark teeth behind. Or maybe I needed to leave a note pinned to my next victim's shirt explaining what happened so these idiots could finally figure it out.

The news anchors hadn't mentioned Kendra's name, but that didn't bother me. All that mattered was her manner of death. She had messed with a shark, and the shark attacked. The same thing happened to Patrice.

I was already getting hungry for my next victim, excited to use my new toy. Night vision goggles.

Sharks have amazingly good eyesight. They can see colors, and they can also see in the dark.

CHAPTER 17

WINTER

Maybe if I were to dig really quickly, everything would be fine. I would only spend a few minutes, maybe five or six, and if nothing was there, then I would hightail it back to the house.

I pulled the mounted flashlight over my head, lacing my ponytail through the back strap, and picked up the shovel. I swung it through the air to feel the weight of it in my hand. This would also serve as my weapon.

I turned on the lantern, but nothing happened. Great. The battery must have died. I left it behind, along with my shoes. Bare feet were the best option for walking in the sand.

When I stepped outside, all I could hear were the thunderous ocean waves roaring in the distance. For some reason they seemed much louder at night. The air was humid and hot like always, but there was a slight breeze that helped make it bearable.

The beam coming from my flashlight wasn't as bright as I had hoped, but that wasn't going to stop me. I angled it toward the ground, wishing I had the sun to guide me. Even the moon would have been helpful.

After I walked through the back gate, I headed toward the roaring ocean shore, which seemed a million miles away. My heart pounded wildly in my chest. My feet struggled with each step as I trudged through the uneven sand. A little voice inside my head kept warning me to go back. Ignoring this urge wasn't easy.

I soon spotted the tall white structure and picked up my pace. Six minutes, I told myself. Only six, not a minute more. I began counting the seconds in my head as I plunged the shovel down into the sand.

I adjusted my grip, about to scoop out the sand, when something wet bumped against my leg. I jumped back, my heart stopping. From the corner of my eye, something zipped past me. I spun around, light darting in every direction with the turn of my head. The darkness hanging in the sky was more than my flashlight could contend with. I couldn't see anything. I froze, trying to listen, wondering if I would be able to hear it. But I couldn't, not with that loud ocean constantly roaring.

I shouldn't have come out here. This was the worst idea I

could have ever had. The ocean had become a sea of darkness, devoid of any beauty or tranquility. It was a raging, powerful entity, with a mind of its own. I was surrounded by sand, which could easily slow down even the fastest of runners. Someone, or something, was out here with me, and I probably wouldn't be able to get away.

My eyes strained to see through the darkness, my hands gripping the shovel handle, holding it up like a baseball bat. I struggled to inhale the heavy, humid air. I listened, trying to discern if there was another noise out there, mixed in with the echoing waves. Then I heard something. It was coming from behind me. I held the shovel at the ready and spun around. Then I saw it. A shadow raced past me, only it was too quick for me to make out what it was. "Who's there?" I shouted. "What do you want?"

I thought I saw movement in the distance again. My feet stumbled backward, and I landed on my butt, the shovel falling from my grasp. Just before I scrambled back up to my feet, a voice spoke and my entire body shook.

"Winter," a deep voice called.

I saw another flash of movement, low to the ground and quick.

"Winter," the same voice called again, only clearer this time. I knew who the voice belonged to now. It was Hunter.

My light pointed directly at the figure standing in front of me. Hunter's black hair and dark clothes blended in with the night sky. Something was different about him. I didn't recognize the eyes staring at me—I had never seen them before. He had always worn sunglasses.

"Winter. Are you okay? It's me, Hunter."

"What are you doing out here?" I gasped.

"I didn't mean to scare you. Are you alone?"

I wasn't comfortable answering his question. He still hadn't answered mine. "What are you doing out here?" I asked him again, my voice shaking.

His expression didn't change. He kept staring blankly. "I was going for a walk."

A walk? Was he by himself, or was Nevin around here somewhere? "Do you always walk around the beach so late at night?"

"Yeah, I do."

I guessed that made sense. It was always dark outside for him, no matter what time of day it was. And at night, he would have the entire beach to himself.

Hunter held out his hand, searchingly. "Max, come here." His big German shepherd suddenly appeared, tongue hanging out of its mouth.

"Is Nevin with you?"

"No." Hunter patted Max's head, then let him go again. "Winter, what are you doing out here?"

Max ran to my side and bumped his wet nose against my leg. I relaxed even more, realizing it was Max who had freaked me out earlier.

"It's not safe to be out here at night by yourself."

"But it's safe for you?"

He shook his head. "I just don't think it's a good idea for you to be out here alone."

"Why?"

"Because you're a girl."

A girl? Did he think I was too weak and vulnerable?

He held up his hand. "I didn't mean it to sound like that—like I'm sexist. I just... How are you going to protect yourself, if somebody tries to attack you?"

"I'm not helpless, Hunter."

He sighed heavily again. "I didn't mean to offend you." There were a few beats of uncomfortable silence. "So do you want to go for a walk together, since we're both out here?"

"I can't. I'm looking for something."

"Do you want me to help?"

He would have to be able to see in order to help me. Then a thought popped into my head. Maybe he could help. "I need to dig a hole and sift through the sand to make sure I don't miss anything. Do you want to sift through the sand?"

"Show me where, and I'll do what I can." He held out his hand, and I led him beneath the lifeguard tower. Hunter sat down and started sifting through the sand, one handful at a time as I started digging.

After several minutes of focused work, he stopped. "How far down are you going to dig?"

I looked down at the gaping hole in front of me, realizing I had probably already dug beyond a reasonable depth. "I think I'm done now."

"Didn't find it, did you?"

"No, I guess it's not here." The hole was deep enough—it had to be. I let go of the shovel, feeling frustrated and defeated. When it landed on the ground, Max sprung to his feet.

"Maybe it's still in this pile somewhere," Hunter suggested, grabbing another handful of sand. "Do you want me to keep searching?"

"I guess it couldn't hurt." I sat down and started sifting through it with him.

"What exactly are we looking for, Winter?"

I probably needed to give him an answer, but I didn't have one. "To tell you the truth, I don't know."

"I figured that you had lost something valuable—something small like a piece of jewelry."

"No. I didn't lose anything. Somebody buried something here."

Hunter lifted his hand and spread apart his fingers, letting the sand fall through. "Who?"

"My aunt Emma."

"She didn't tell you what she buried?" He looked toward me, but his gaze missed my eyes.

"No, she never got the chance. I'm not even sure she buried it."

"So it's still in your house somewhere?"

Was it still in the house? I thought about Tamara going

through Aunt Emma's bedroom. Was she looking for the mystery item? Did she find it? "I just wish I knew what it was."

Hunter stood up and brushed off his hands. "Maybe it's one of those things where once you find it, you just know."

"Yeah, wouldn't that be nice?" If only it could be that easy.

CHAPTER 18

WINTER

After Hunter and I filled the hole back in, he wished me luck, told me to let him know if I ever did find what I was looking for, and then he urged me to go back inside the house right away so I would be safe. Instead of getting irritated with him again, I just told him I planned on it. Then he and Max wandered off down the beach.

As I approached my house, I found myself strangely still enveloped in darkness. Both the interior and exterior house lights had been turned off. When I tried to open the back door, I was met with something else unexpected. It was locked!

I quickly walked around to the front of the house. Mom's and Tim's vehicles were both gone. The old SUV sat there by itself looking as useless as it was ugly in the haze of intermittent passing headlights. I didn't have a key to the SUV or to the house.

After ringing the doorbell at least fifty times and pounding on its hard surface until my hands ached, I decided to search for another way in. The garage door, both side doors, and all of the windows were locked. There wasn't one loose screen, rickety door, or strategically placed spare key anywhere.

Then it dawned on me that it was Friday night. Tim and Tamara probably wouldn't get home until late. And as for Mom, I had no idea when she would return home. She usually went out on the weekends, but I didn't think she'd go anywhere tonight with a headache.

Even though I was almost positive that nobody was home, I made my way back around to the front of the house and gave the doorbell a couple more tries. The echoing chime sounded faintly in my ears. Nobody came.

I knew that I had left the back door unlocked. I even checked it twice. Mom couldn't have locked it. Her philosophy has always been that if someone wanted to break into our house, they were gonna break in. They would just kick down the door or break a window. Either way, they would get in if they wanted. So she never locked the doors. I always had to do it.

Tamara couldn't have locked me out. She was already gone when I left to go to the beach. So it had to have been Tim. Who did he think he was? He wasn't the man of this house. He was just a renter, and he better not forget that.

As I sat on the steps of the front porch, a sudden gust of wind blew through the air, sending a few loose strands of my hair into my face. I shivered and crossed my arms over my chest. It was hot out tonight, but I still felt a chill go through me. The trees and bushes fluttered and swayed, filling the air with strange noises. Once in a while a car drove by much slower than the speed limit. I wondered if whoever was driving by was watching me.

The spookiness of this night was rising to a level unlike any I had ever experienced. And I had lived in some pretty scary places before, around some seriously sketchy people. But everything felt different for me now, because of Aunt Emma's death and that threatening letter. I wondered if Mom and I were in some kind of danger.

After another slow-moving vehicle drove by, I decided to go back out to the beach and look for Hunter. As I walked along the shore, I stayed close to the ocean and far away from all of the hiding places near the houses. I called Hunter's name over and over. He didn't have a flashlight for me to spot shining off in the distance. He had dark hair, wore dark clothes, and blended right in with the night sky. My chances of finding him seemed slim to none, but I hoped I would get lucky—if that was even possible.

I began heading in the direction of the pier. All of the businesses stayed open late down there. Maybe that was where Hunter was.

Most of the sand I walked across was smooth and soft, except for the occasional rough patches full of broken seashells that crept up on me, jabbing into the flesh on the bottom of my feet. The cool ocean water stretched out, covering the path I walked. If the water ever hit me higher than my ankles, I moved away from it.

After what seemed like an eternity, I finally made it to the pier. The glow of its dim lights invited me in.

When my feet finally landed on wood planks, I pulled the head-mounted light off and began searching for Hunter among the crowd. Near the end of the pier, I saw Jaxson standing there with a group of guys. He was wearing a backward baseball cap and a Carolina Panthers football jersey. I looked around for Eli but didn't see him anywhere. Then another familiar face in the crowd caught my attention. It was Nevin. He wasn't wearing his usual baseball cap or sunglasses. His red hair had an orangish hue to it under the glow of the lights. He noticed me staring at him and waved. "Hey," he called out.

Jaxson turned around and saw me. He leaned into Nevin, whispering something in his ear.

Nevin nodded, then motioned for me to come over. "Winter," he called out. "Come here!"

I wasn't interested in hanging out with them. I wanted to find Hunter.

I continued walking past them at a quicker pace. When I arrived at the end of the pier, I had nowhere else to go and there was still no sign of Hunter. Crap! I thought for sure I would find him. I did not want to have to turn around and pass by Jaxson and Nevin again.

In an effort to sneak by unnoticed, I slipped in with a small cluster of preteen girls, hoping to blend in.

Just as I was about to pass Nevin and Jaxson, an eruption of loud voices filled the air. I immediately stopped when I saw Nevin fighting with someone. Fists were flying, and they were up against the railing. Somehow Nevin got ahold of the guy, lifting him up onto the railing. Was he going to throw him over the edge into the ocean? I watched in horror as the guy struggled to break free, but Nevin already had him partway over the railing.

The guy yelled out, and somehow Nevin grabbed him by his legs, holding him upside down, dangling headfirst over the side. All of the other guys in their group, including Jaxson, were laughing, urging Nevin to drop him.

"Pull me back up!"

"Jaxson, come here!" Nevin called, glancing over his shoulder. "Grab his shoes."

What was Nevin doing? Why did he want his shoes?

Jaxson yanked the shoes off the helpless guy's feet and tossed them into the ocean. "If you want those back," Jaxson taunted, "you're gonna have to swim for them."

"Pull me up!" came the panicked reply.

"Are you going to do as I say?" Nevin yelled down at him.

I didn't know if I should intervene or if that would only make things worse. I looked over the railing. Violent ocean waves crashed against the tall posts of the pier. It was so dark down there.

"Answer the question!" Nevin yelled.

"Yes, I'll listen to you! I swear!"

Nevin finally pulled the guy back up and gave him a shove, knocking him to the ground.

Jaxson stood there laughing mockingly, his white teeth glowing in the dim lights on the pier. "You're lucky. I would have let you fall."

I took off and didn't look back, hoping Jaxson and Nevin hadn't seen me.

I pulled the mounted light back onto my head. But when I clicked the button, nothing happened. Crap! I turned from the beach and headed toward the road instead, walking fast. I passed the restaurants, the people, the bars...until the sidewalk came to an end and the long stretch of road began.

There weren't any more streetlights, just porch lights and occasional headlights from passing cars. I walked along the bike lane, my bare feet contending with rocks and other road debris.

Some of the stretches of road were darker than others, and I found myself surrounded by thick vegetation. Occasionally leaves would continue to shake, even after the wind gusts died down. My biggest fear was that someone would be hiding in one of those dark places—behind the trees and bushes—and they would be watching me, following me.

With each set of approaching headlights, my heart rate sped up. What if someone were to stop their vehicle and throw me into the trunk of their car? Or what if they followed me home? What if Nevin or Jaxson was in one of those cars?

The next big gust of wind made the leaves rustle and shake, sending strange noises into the air. I tried to ignore the movements in the shadows and the cars that drove by way too slow and instead focused on getting home. If my guess was correct, I still had about a mile to go.

A faint rumbling noise started up, coming from somewhere behind me. At first I thought it was thunder, but the noise was too constant. Was it some kind of animal growling? I turned around and walked backward a few steps but didn't see anything. The noise suddenly grew louder. Adrenaline shot through my entire body. I spun back around and took off running.

My heart hammered in my chest as my feet pounded against the pavement. House after house I pressed my pace until my lungs were stinging. With one last dark lot to pass, I lengthened my stride. I gasped for air, breathing so hard that I could no longer hear the noises around me. I could see my house. Mom's car was still gone, but Tim's truck was there!

I ran across the small patch of grass in our front yard, my legs feeling heavy as I raced up the steps to the front porch. I mashed the doorbell repeatedly and pounded on the door. Why wasn't Tim answering?

Just as another set of headlights approached on the road, I turned around and took off back down the porch steps. I headed around to the back of the house, then through the side gate to Hunter's, hoping he was home. I pounded on the door. Nobody answered, so I turned to leave.

As I reached for the latch on the gate, it swung open on its own. I jumped back and inhaled, about to scream.

"Who's there?" a husky voice called from somewhere in the dark.

Then I saw him. "Hunter, you scared me!"

"I'm sorry. I didn't know you were there." He rested his hand on the fence post, eyes staring off into the darkness. "Is everything okay?"

"I've been looking everywhere for you."

"You have?" Hunter's voice cracked slightly.

"Yeah." I pointed, forgetting that visual cues were useless. "I'm locked out of my house."

He stepped through the gate. "Well, come on in."

Hunter opened the back door without a key. Apparently he had left it unlocked. Max poked his head out to greet us. That was when I realized something wasn't right. Hunter didn't have his cane or Max to guide him. He must have brought Max to the house and then headed back to the beach without him.

How was he able to walk around out there by himself? Was he with somebody? If so, who? It couldn't have been Nevin. He was at the pier. How did he find his way home alone? And why had he come back out without Max?

CHAPTER 19

WINTER

Hunter's house was thick with darkness and smelled like bleach. I searched along the walls for light switches and turned them on as we passed through the family room and the living room. His house was decorated like a typical beach house: blue furniture, flooring the color of the sand, decorative seashells, pictures of the ocean hanging on the walls. It was bright and cheerful.

I followed him up the stairs, and we entered a large game room. There was a pool table, a foosball table, a Skee-Ball arcade game, a wet bar, and an enormous flat-screen TV, much bigger than the TV at my house.

"Wow," I said. "Is this your man cave?"

"The house was already furnished when I moved in."

I walked over to the foosball table and gave the handle a spin. "The only thing that seems to be missing is a bowling alley."

Hunter sat down on the brown leather sectional and reclined his seat back. Max found a spot on the floor below him.

I was still wondering how he was able to find his way around outside tonight without Max or his cane. Maybe Hunter really wasn't blind. "I was looking for you out on the beach," I said as I surveyed Hunter's face, waiting for his reaction. "I headed in the same direction that you went, but it was like you vanished into thin air. Where did you go?"

He shrugged, his expression blank. "We must have just missed each other somehow."

I really wanted to know what he was doing out there and where he had gone. When did he bring Max back to his house? And why? "I walked all the way to the pier. I didn't see you anywhere."

Hunter's eyes shifted, missing mine, and his brow furrowed. "You shouldn't go down to the pier late at night by yourself. It's not safe."

"What's wrong with going to the pier?"

"There are some people who hang out down there that you don't want to get involved with. Trust me." He laced his fingers behind his head and crossed his ankles.

I thought about that fight Nevin got into. Was Hunter talking about Nevin? But Nevin worked for him. Why would he warn me about someone he trusted enough to help him on a daily basis? Maybe he was referring to Jaxson, or maybe he was talking about another group of people. "I saw Nevin and Jaxson down at the pier. Do you know Jaxson?"

Hunter suddenly sat forward. A deep crease appeared between his eyebrows. "Nevin was there?"

"Yeah. He got into a fight. He almost threw some guy off the pier. He held him by his legs, dangling him over the railing, about to drop him into the ocean, then he told Jaxson to pull his shoes off and throw them in the ocean. He eventually pulled the guy back up, and then he knocked him to the ground."

Hunter shifted in his seat, his jaw tensed. "I'm gonna have a talk with Nevin. He knows better than to hang out with them. Was Eli there too?"

"No, he wasn't there. But if he would've been, I'm sure he would have stopped Nevin from terrorizing that guy."

Hunter's brows knit together. He placed his feet on the floor like he was going to stand up, but he didn't. "Are you kidding me? Wow. Eli must really have you fooled. That guy is the worst of all of them. He's the one you should stay away from."

What? Eli was responsible, kind, and friendly. He had been nothing but nice to me, and I hadn't picked up on any strange vibes from him—nothing that would make me think he was untrustworthy or trouble. "What's wrong with Eli? Why should I stay away from him?"

Hunter picked at a thread that had come loose from the arm of the couch, the crease firmly set between his eyebrows. "He's reckless and dangerous. He's done some things in his past that are unforgivable."

Unforgivable? That's extreme. "What did he do?"

"He abused his brother. He traumatized—" Hunter stopped mid-sentence, forcefully strumming his fingers on the arm of the couch. "I don't want to talk about that right now."

I sat there, confused. I couldn't imagine Eli hurting anybody. Maybe there was more to the story that Hunter didn't know about. Or maybe Eli had changed, grown up and matured, and was no longer that kind of person. "Was this recent? Or was it a long time ago?"

"It doesn't matter how long ago it was. What matters is it happened. He's not the person you think he is. Don't fool yourself into believing that he's someone you can trust."

"Hunter, you can't just drop a bomb like that and then be all secretive about the details."

Hunter shook his head. "The details don't matter. All that matters is what I told you."

"If it doesn't matter, then why did you bring it up at all?"

"Well, I shouldn't have. So just forget about it." Hunter stood up and walked over to the mini fridge. He pulled out two bottles of water. "Do you want some water?"

"No." What I wanted was for him to tell me what happened. What did Eli do? "Hunter, I told you why I was out on the beach tonight digging under the lifeguard tower. That wasn't something I'd tell just anybody. It was my secret, and I trusted you enough to tell you about it. Why can't you trust me and tell me what Eli did?"

He put the extra bottle of water back inside the fridge.

"Winter, I told you everything that you need to know. Stay away from Eli, and stay away from the pier at night, because that's where he hangs out."

"So you're not going to tell me?" I asked, irritated.

"No," he said firmly, then he unscrewed the lid of his water and took a drink.

I couldn't deal with Hunter anymore tonight—I'd had enough. My patience was gone. "I better go check to see if my mom's home now." I got up from the couch, stepped over Max, and was about to pass by Hunter when he moved in front of the door, blocking my path.

"You just got here." His lips twitched like he was going to say something else, but he stopped.

"I need to go home." I moved around to his right. He simultaneously turned, and our bodies collided. I stumbled, crashing into the wall with my shoulder. Somehow Hunter remained standing firmly in place.

"Are you okay?" he asked. "I'm so sorry."

I had given him plenty of room. We shouldn't have collided like that. Did he deliberately bump into me? "I'm fine," I snapped, holding my shoulder.

"I really am sorry. I didn't mean to run into you. Winter, if you're still locked out and can't get back into your house, you're welcome to stay the night here. I've got plenty of extra bedrooms for you to choose from. And I am really sorry about bumping into you."

My shoulder was sore, and I couldn't get the thought out

of my head that he might have knocked me over on purpose. I didn't want to believe it, but his movements seemed so intentional.

"I'm sure I'll be able to get into my house now—my mom should be home," I lied, making a beeline for the door. I walked quickly down the hallway, hoping he wasn't following me. When I got downstairs, I ran through his house, straight to the back door. I moved quickly through his backyard and slammed the gate shut behind me.

When I arrived at the front of my house, I discovered that Mom's car was still gone, which was what I had expected. I just wanted to get away from Hunter, even if that meant I had to stay outside by myself all night long.

I began ringing the doorbell over and over, hoping that Tim would wake up.

Still no luck.

I sat down on the steps and watched the cars driving by, my thoughts shifting to the things Hunter said about Eli.

I had already learned the hard way not to believe one person's version of the truth without giving the other person involved a chance to explain their side too. I had made the mistake of not checking the facts when Chaz told me that Venus had dumped him for a guy that I liked. Chaz had been lying, but I didn't know that. He sounded so convincing.

I felt betrayed by Venus. Part of me was already jealous of her, because she was prettier than me, and she turned the heads of almost every guy at school. So the story Chaz told me was easy for me to believe.

But it turned out that there was no cheating involved at all. Venus had gotten tired of Chaz controlling and manipulating her. I never should have listened to him.

Another car drove by, music blaring, bass thumping, and I set those thoughts aside, ready to try the doorbell again. The music from the car eventually faded. There was silence, except for the faint ringing of the doorbell. Then I heard the lock click.

Tim opened the door. He was standing there in his bathrobe with his hairy chest exposed. "Got locked out, huh?" he chuckled.

I didn't find the humor in this. I burst through the door, walking right past him, then stopped just before going up the stairs. I turned back around to face him. "Do you know where my mom is?"

He pointed toward the back of the house. "She left a note on the fridge."

I headed to the kitchen to read the note.

Winter,
I had to go help my friend Cari. Her car broke down in Virginia. I probably won't be home till late tomorrow.

Love,
Mom

I crumpled up the note and tossed it into the trash.

Tim was sitting in front of the TV with his knees spread apart, his robe on the brink of bursting open. I hoped he was wearing shorts under there. He was holding a huge mixing bowl full of cereal, a wooden serving spoon in his hand.

"Why didn't you answer the door earlier?" I asked him.

He turned his head to look at me, milk dripping from his chin. "Huh?"

"About a half hour ago."

He nodded, finally understanding me. "I was probably in the shower." He shrugged like it wasn't a big deal.

His lack of concern only infuriated me more. I exhaled forcefully, rolling my eyes. But he didn't notice. He was already watching TV again.

Tim was a loner, didn't have any kids, and didn't have a girlfriend—as far as I knew anyway. All he did was work, eat, and make messes in the kitchen. But still, I wanted him to act like he cared. Was I expecting too much? I didn't think so.

I couldn't stop myself from being angry at him and everybody else. I was mad at Hunter for not trusting me and for plowing into me—accident or not. I was mad at Mom for being a notoriously absent mother and for not caring about Aunt Emma's death. She had barely acknowledged the suspicious letter. I was mad at Tamara. She was a liar, and she was evil. Whatever was buried under the lifeguard tower had already been taken, probably by her. She was likely the one who wrote that letter and killed Aunt Emma. If not, she was at least involved somehow. Anger continued to boil inside me. I felt so out of control of everything in my life.

"Tim," I snapped. "Are you the one who locked the back door earlier tonight?"

He turned and looked at me, brow furrowed, then swallowed his mouthful of cereal. "I didn't get home from work until about an hour ago," he replied, defensively.

I wanted to be mad at Tim and blame him for everything I had been through tonight, but now I couldn't. Maybe Mom was the one who locked me out. But that seemed so unlike her. She had never been cautious and careful before.

I knew that she loved me, but she wasn't a responsible mother. She had always let me do whatever I wanted. I could stay out all night, even on a school night, and I could have anybody sleep over. When I dropped out of school, she didn't seem upset or disappointed. She never once lectured me. She was more like a friend than a mother.

I went straight upstairs and climbed right into bed, but I was unable to fall asleep.

There was a time when Mom and I were homeless. I had just turned eight when Mom lost her job. We had to live in our beat-up old SUV during the middle of the summer for three long, hot weeks.

When Aunt Emma found out, she moved back to Utah and invited us to live with her in her travel trailer. It wasn't the best situation since we were so cramped for space, but we did have a bed to sleep in and a roof over our heads.

Then one day, Aunt Emma's ex-boyfriend came pounding on the door, wanting his trailer back. I couldn't really remember much else about what happened that day, except for the cops showing up. The next memory I had was of us moving into an apartment. Aunt Emma lived with us in that same apartment until Kyle died.

I closed my eyes, rolled over onto my stomach, and soon thoughts about my past vanished from my mind.

CHAPTER 20

WINTER

The next morning, I started searching through the garage, opening boxes and storage bins, looking through drawers and cupboards. I wondered if Hunter's theory might be correct. Maybe I would find the item that Aunt Emma was supposed to have buried somewhere in the house. Since the garage was part of the house, I thought I would start there.

After several hours of searching, all I had found was a bunch of random junk, none of which looked like it belonged to Aunt Emma. This was all Reginald's old stuff: clothes, trophies, yearbooks, anything and everything computer related like keyboards, monitors, wires, hard drives, and other things that looked like they belonged inside a computer to make it work.

I found one of his old fishing poles and a tackle box full of supplies: hooks, fishing line, and lures. I remembered Mom had told me that my father loved going fishing. I had never gone fishing before but wondered if I would enjoy it too.

On a whim, I decided to postpone my search for another day and head down to the pier, pole and tackle box in hand.

When I walked outside, the sun immediately began beating down on my shoulders, arms, and legs, while my face remained mostly shaded by my baseball cap. I was glad I remembered to put on some sunscreen.

Just like yesterday, most of the people on the beach were hovering close to shore. Only a few brave swimmers dared to go out into the deep water. Hopefully they wouldn't end up as shark bait.

After a long, and extremely hot and sweaty walk, I finally arrived at the pier. I sat on a bench with my supplies watching a brown pelican perched on top of a post a few feet away. His huge shovel of a beak remained tucked in close to his long skinny neck. Whenever people got too close, he would quickly fly to another perch farther away, then return after they had gone.

There were about a dozen other people out here fishing. They all looked like they knew what they were doing, with their multiple fishing poles and ice chests at the ready. I was by far the youngest and of course the least experienced. It took me about five tries before I was able to cast my line into the water, and even then it didn't go far.

If by some freak chance a fish did decide to take a bite

of my bright pink lure, I hoped that one of these more seasoned fishermen would help me so that I could toss it back into the water. I actually didn't want to catch anything, I just wanted to know if I could. I didn't like the taste of fish. Well, except for shrimp. But it had to be breaded and fried.

An older man in a red hat shuffled past me, fishing gear in tow. He had a bristly, walrus-like mustache and wore a shiny silver watch. "Having any luck, little lady?" he asked me.

"Nope, not yet."

He quickly cast his line out into the water, then began preparing a second fishing pole.

Far out in the ocean, and all by itself, a boat sped across the water. I continued to watch it for several minutes, until it eventually disappeared.

The man with the mustache noticed it too. "Fishing on a boat..." He nodded toward the open water. "Now that's the best way to go fishing, as long as you don't get seasick." He winked and smiled, but I couldn't see his teeth with all that hair on his upper lip.

"I've never been on a boat before," I admitted.

"I used to be in the navy. I spent eight years on a ship, and I still love the sea. Never got seasick once—" He stopped talking mid-sentence, stood up, and grabbed his fishing pole with both hands. "That was fast."

I leaned forward, looking between the wood slats of the railing down at the water below.

"Whatever this is, it's big!" he said loudly, drawing the attention of other people nearby.

I kept my eyes fixed on the choppy, blue-gray water, waiting for his big fish to surface.

The rate of his reeling eventually began to slow. He seemed to be struggling but remained focused on his eagerly anticipated catch. "Daggum! This thing weighs a ton."

"What kind of fish do you think it is?" I asked.

"I don't know, little lady... I don't know."

Finally the fish came into view just below the water's surface. It was definitely big and looked to be light in color, almost like it was glowing under the water. "There it is." I pointed.

"What in the Sam Hill..." The man's eyes squinted as he leaned over the railing.

I moved closer to get a better look. A couple other people gathered around, with more heading our way. An older woman stood next to me, peering down over the railing. Her warm hand clamped down onto my arm as she let out a loud scream. I jumped back, covering my ear.

"What is it?" someone shouted.

The man with the mustache almost dropped his pole. "Call 911!" he yelled.

I blinked in disbelief, my breath catching. At the end of his fishing line, floating partially above the choppy sea water, was another dead girl. Or was she still alive? Her long brown hair and a pink flowing dress were tangled in seaweed. She wasn't moving—at least I didn't think she was.

It was too dangerous to jump into the water from all the way up here—not that I was going to do that. But I wondered if somebody else would—someone who was a better swimmer than me.

"I'm on the phone with the 911 dispatcher," a voice shouted. "Help is on the way."

What if that takes too long? What if the girl dies before help arrives?

The older lady next to me began screaming into her phone. "There's a body in the water!"

The man with the mustache kept one hand on his fishing pole, the other on his chest. He quickly muttered something under his breath, then grasped both hands firmly onto his fishing pole again.

I wasn't sure if the girl in the water was floating face down. Was her head turned with her mouth and nose slightly above the water? It was too difficult to see clearly from this height, and her long brown hair was all over her face.

I ran back down to shore, wondering if I could help, but her body was unreachable, floating far beyond the crashing waves. A lifeguard came running past me. He swam out to the girl but only stayed there for a few seconds before turning back around and swimming to shore. The look on his face could only be described as sheer horror. He buckled over, vomit spewing out of his mouth.

My question had been answered. The girl was dead.

When the police arrived, they cleared the pier and the

surrounding beach area. I had left my fishing gear up there with my line still in the water, and now I couldn't go back to get it.

This section of the beach was much busier than the area behind my house. The number of onlookers continued to increase by the minute. Several lifeguards huddled together next to the taped-off area. Both Eli and Jaxson were there. I also saw Nevin again. He was working his EMT job.

If this girl had been attacked by a shark, I wondered if a bunch of fishermen would go out on their boats to hunt for the creature. But maybe three victims weren't enough to warrant such actions, or maybe they only did that kind of thing in movies.

Time continued to pass, and the heat was becoming unbearable. The extreme dryness of my throat and mouth was almost painful. I had stayed among the crowd of onlookers for way too long, holding on to the notion that at any minute I would find out what had happened to the girl. It was time for me to call it a day.

As I turned to leave, the next person behind me pushed forward, quickly taking my spot.

The older woman who had screamed in my ear earlier on the pier was sitting nearby in a chair. She waved me down. I almost continued walking past her, but I decided to stop for just a minute and see what she wanted.

"Did you hear what happened to her?" she asked.

I cleared my throat. "No. Did you?"

"I talked to one of the lifeguards, that blond one right there." She pointed at Jaxson. "He said it was another shark attack. They found a couple of shark teeth left behind. It's not safe to go swimming in the water. They should close the beaches right now."

"I agree," I replied as I started walking away. "Thanks for letting me know. I'll be sure to stay clear of the water." My energy level continued to decline, so I had to get moving.

My curiosity had been satisfied. I had found out what happened, and I wasn't surprised.

My return trip home required that I walk along the shore. All these shark attacks had me spooked, but I was also baking to death from the sun. I made a compromise and allowed myself to keep my feet in the water to cool off, but never let it go higher than my ankles.

The beach seemed like it stretched on forever, and my energy level continued to diminish. I knew I was in trouble when my vision started to dim. I stopped and sat down, only it was too late. Everything around me went black.

CHAPTER 21

WINTER

My eyes were shut, and I didn't have the strength to open them. There was a grittiness in my mouth. My clothes felt wet. I knew I had passed out. I just didn't know for how long.

"Are you okay?" a high-pitched voice asked, waves roaring in the background.

"What happened?" I heard someone else ask.

More voices filled the air. None of them sounded familiar.

"Can you hear me?" a deep voice shouted.

Finally I managed to pry my heavy eyelids open. At first it was difficult to see what was going on around me. The sun was too bright. Then I saw faces. They were all staring at me. A hand reached behind my back to steady me as I sat up. Salt water came rushing over my legs.

"Here you go, hun." A bottle of water was shoved into my

chest. A silver-haired woman pushed her sunglasses on top of her head. Mascara had smeared under her eyes. "It's extremely hot out today. You probably need to cool down and hydrate."

I took a couple sips of water. It ran down my throat, mixing with the sand in my mouth.

Another woman brushed my hair off my shoulder and out of my face. "Sweetie. Are you feeling okay now?"

"Of course she's not okay," the silver-haired woman replied for me. "She needs an ambulance."

I pulled the water bottle from my mouth and swallowed quickly, almost choking. "No. I don't need an ambulance."

"Who's here with you? Where are they?" The silver-haired woman looked around. "I can go get them for you."

"You don't need to go get anybody," I insisted.

The two women looked at each other, then the silver-haired woman stood up, placing her hand on her hip. "I wonder when those lifeguards are going to get here."

I shook my head. "I don't need a lifeguard either."

"I sent my son to go get them," someone behind me said. "They should be here soon."

When I started to get up, the silver-haired woman dropped down to her knees, waving her hands. "Hold on now."

The other woman grabbed my arm. "You need to stay put. Help is on the way."

If I had the energy, I would've gotten up right then. But I still felt a little dizzy. I heard an engine approaching and hoped it wasn't an EMT or a lifeguard heading this way.

Another water bottle was offered to me, even though I hadn't finished the first one. Then I was offered a bag of chips and some cookies. The crowd that had gathered around me parted when the sound of the engine cut off.

"Winter?"

I turned and looked, wondering if my ears had deceived me. But no. It was Eli.

"Look who it is," Jaxson announced, suddenly appearing at my side. "The snow queen."

Snow queen? Great, he had given me a nickname—a terrible nickname.

Eli kneeled down next to me, his dark eyes searching my face. "What happened? Are you all right?" He didn't sound panicked, just concerned.

The two women taking care of me told him everything. I didn't have to say a word. All of this attention was absolutely embarrassing.

Eli took hold of my arm and pressed his fingers to the inside of my wrist. His touch left a trail of goose bumps up my arm.

Jaxson had a sly grin on his face. "Too bad you don't need CPR." He cupped his hand over his mouth, exhaled, then sniffed his breath. "Yep, my breath is good. Spearmint gum. You missed out." He laughed.

CPR was probably Jaxson's best chance at actually kissing a girl.

Eli removed his fingers from my wrist. "Your pulse is fine." He shot Jaxson a look of irritation. Then he turned his attention back to me again. "Winter, you should probably get checked out by a doctor, just to be on the safe side."

I didn't have health insurance or the extra money to pay for any medical bills, so I couldn't go to the doctor. I knew Eli was just doing his job by suggesting this, but I hoped he would drop the subject.

"You really should listen to his advice," Jaxson said, nodding in agreement.

"I am fine," I insisted. "My blood sugar was low, and I just needed some water. I'm good. Seriously. I'll go home and make sure to take it easy for the rest of the day."

"Let me at least drive you to your house," Eli said.

Drive me? "Okay," I quickly agreed. He didn't have to ask me twice. I did not want to walk the rest of the way home.

Eli stretched out his hand to help me up, but Jaxson got to me first. He held my arm to keep me from falling, but I wasn't losing my balance and his extra assistance was not necessary. Still, he held on as he led me over to the ATV and then climbed in the back seat next to me.

"You know, if I had saved your life, then you would've owed me," Jaxson said with a sly grin.

I stared at him, unimpressed with his humor.

"So where did you disappear to last night?" he asked as the engine rumbled to life.

"Nowhere. I went home," I replied in a low voice, hoping he'd drop the subject. Why did he even want to know?

Jaxson nodded, smiling wide with his big white teeth. He

leaned forward to Eli. "You should've been there, brah. A bunch of us were at the pier last night. Then Winter walks up and Nevin was like, *hey girl, come on over here.*" Jaxson smacked his hands together. "Then Winter took off. She was outta there, brah," he said, laughing. "It was hilarious. She made Nevin look like a fool, rejecting him like that."

I buried my face in my hands. Shut up, Jaxson! It wasn't like that. I didn't reject Nevin. I just didn't want to talk to him.

"Winter?"

I removed my hands from my face.

Eli had craned his neck to look at me. "Are you okay?"

"I'm fine." And I wasn't lying. I really was feeling better.

When we arrived at my house, they both followed me inside. Eli went to the kitchen and poured me a glass of water. I headed straight to the couch and sat down. Jaxson stood there doing nothing useful, which was probably his standard mode of operation in life.

"Hey, brah," Jaxson said to Eli. "I'll stay here with her and make sure she's okay." He plopped down on the couch next to me, and I almost spilled the glass of water that Eli had just handed to me.

"Jaxson, watch out," I grumbled, holding the glass away from me so it wouldn't spill.

"Oops, my bad." He chuckled.

Eli stood in front of Jaxson with his arms folded across his chest. "You need to take the ATV back to Patrick before he fires you."

"Freakin' Patrick," Jaxson grumbled, springing to his feet. "I'll see you later, Winter." He hurdled over the couch and took off out the back door.

"Don't you need to get back to work too?" I asked Eli, hoping he didn't.

"Jaxson can cover for me. I don't want to leave you here alone until I know that you're all right. Is your mom here?" He turned to look down the hallway.

"She went to Virginia to help a friend who had car trouble." I knew I would be fine and that Eli really didn't need to stay with me. My energy seemed to be back to normal. But I had already told him that I was fine, and I wasn't going to insist that he leave, not when he wanted to stay.

"Is anybody else here? What about your dad?"

"I don't think anyone else is home. It's just me, my mom, and two renters who live here. You know Tamara, and then there's a guy named Tim."

Eli sat down next to me, and all I kept thinking was how wrong Hunter was about him. Eli couldn't be the monster that Hunter portrayed him to be. He couldn't have been abusive to his brother. That didn't make sense.

"I talked to Hunter last night," I said, unsure how to bring up the subject, so I just jumped straight to the point. "He said I should stay away from you."

Eli's eyes narrowed. "Why?"

"He said that you terrorized and abused your brother

and that you had done something else unforgivable, but he wouldn't tell me what you did."

Eli turned to face me, giving me direct eye contact. "I have never abused my brother. I hope you don't believe that story, because that's all it is. A story. It isn't true."

"I know. I believe you. The whole thing sounded weird." I picked up my glass of water and stared down at the ice inside. "I kind of feel stupid for bringing it up."

"Well, you shouldn't. I'd rather you tell me than keep it to yourself. There's nothing to feel stupid about."

I appreciated him saying that. It helped me feel a little bit better. But now how do I change the subject and move on from this without being totally awkward? The first thing I could think of was popcorn. "I'm hungry. Do you want some popcorn?" I got up from the couch and headed to the kitchen.

"I can get it if you want. You don't have to do it."

"No, you stay there. I'll be right back."

I popped some popcorn in the microwave and brought back two cans of Pepsi. Thankfully the conversation moved on to less serious things.

Eli told me about being part of the robotics club at school, how he wanted to study engineering in college. I told him that Mom was going to college at UNC Wilmington. I didn't know what I wanted to study in college, but I knew that I wanted to go. A college degree would be my best chance at avoiding having to work for minimum wage the rest of my life. I had already worked a couple different fast-food jobs.

As we sat there and talked, I kept wondering if Jaxson would come barging through the door looking for Eli. I was feeling guilty about keeping him from his job. "Is your boss going to wonder where you are?" I asked.

"Naw. Jaxson is covering for me. He owes me." Eli leaned his head back against the couch but kept his eyes locked on to mine. Our hands were almost touching. Then his phone chimed.

"Do you need to get that?"

"It's probably Jaxson. He's just gonna have to wait."

I smiled in response. I couldn't deny that I liked how he had just dropped everything else he had going on today so that he could be here with me.

We talked for a little while longer. I kept expecting him to leave, but he didn't, despite his phone going off three more times. Not only was I anticipating Jaxson barging in on us, I was wondering if Tamara would suddenly appear, strutting around in her tiny bikini. But she still hadn't come home.

"What were you doing down at the pier?" Eli asked.

"Last night?"

He raised his eyebrows. "I was referring to today, but what happened last night? What was Jaxson talking about?"

"I saw Jaxson, Nevin, and a group of their friends. But I didn't run away from Nevin," I clarified. *Or did I?* I couldn't remember if I ran or if I just walked fast. Whatever. It didn't matter. "Nevin got into a fight with some guy and held him over the edge of the pier like he was going to drop him."

"What were they fighting about?" Eli picked up his Pepsi and took a drink.

"I have no idea."

"You went down to the pier again today, right?" He reached into the bowl of popcorn, grabbing a handful.

"Yeah. I was fishing off the pier when that girl's body was found. I was standing right next to the guy who hooked her on his fishing line. And then I waited around to find out what happened to her. I heard it was another shark attack."

Eli set his Pepsi down. "I heard the same thing."

"So, I was wondering… When a shark attacks someone, aren't they usually able to swim away? They may lose a limb or a lot of blood, but don't they normally survive?" I took a drink of my Pepsi, waiting for his response.

"Yeah. It depends on the size and type of shark, but generally that's true, around here anyway."

"So why did those girls die?"

He shook his head. "I don't think a shark is to blame."

I set my Pepsi down on the coffee table, giving him my full attention. "If a shark isn't to blame, then what killed them?"

"It's more like, who?" he replied. "I think a serial killer is responsible for their deaths."

A serial killer… I turned and looked out the window, a lump forming in my throat. The massive ocean loomed in the distance, the blue sky hovering above, and the soft, billowy sand below. Who would come to a place like this and start killing people? Who would do something so unthinkable?

The front door slammed shut, followed by quick footsteps moving up the stairs.

"Is that your mom?"

"Sounds more like Tamara," I replied.

A steady clicking noise filled the air, continuing to grow louder. I had no idea what the sound was coming from until Hunter walked around the corner with Max. I sat up straight, worried Hunter would freak out when he learned that Eli was here. And what was Eli going to do? Was he going to confront Hunter for lying about him?

"Hey, Hunter," I said, hesitating, unsure how to tell him that Eli was in the room. He was going to find out sooner or later, and it was better if he found out sooner.

"Hey," he replied, pushing his sunglasses up on his nose. "Tamara said I should just come in. I hope you don't mind. I know things didn't end well the last time we hung out together. I wanted to apologize. I probably shouldn't have told you that stuff about Eli."

The blood drained from my face. I had waited too long. I should have interrupted him.

"Winter," Eli said. "I better get going. Do you think you're gonna be all right?"

I could see the tension in Eli's neck and jaw. Maybe it was a good idea for him to leave. "Yeah, I'll be fine. Thank you so much for helping me today."

He nodded then quickly slipped outside. Before walking away, he looked back through the glass door at Hunter.

"Why didn't you tell me he was here?" Hunter asked.

"I'm sorry, I didn't get a chance. I didn't know you were going to mention his name."

Hunter's fingers gripped tightly around Max's harness. He took a deep breath like he was trying to calm himself down. "Is he your…boyfriend?"

That was really none of his business, and I didn't want to hear another lecture about how horrible Eli was. "Why don't you have a seat? Can I get you a drink or something to eat?" I directed Hunter over to the couch.

"I'm sorry," he said as he sat down. "I didn't know you were seeing each other. You're probably mad at me, aren't you?"

Why was he still talking about him? "Eli and I are not seeing each other, and I'm not mad," I said, hoping he would drop the subject.

"Just promise me one thing."

Okay, this was getting old. My patience was running thin. "What's on your mind, Hunter?"

He shook his head. "It was nothing. Just a random thought, but it doesn't matter. Forget it."

I felt certain he wanted me to promise him something about Eli. I was glad he dropped the subject instead.

I picked up the remote and turned on the TV, but I kept the volume muted.

"Did something happen to you, Winter?"

"What do you mean?"

"Eli had asked if you were all right."

I explained to Hunter what had happened today at the pier with the dead body and how I had passed out. Just as I finished telling him the story, the news came on the TV. They were showing footage of the pier. I turned the volume up.

The news anchor said that today's victim lived in Wilmington with two roommates. She was eighteen and had recently graduated from the local high school. Her name was Lauraine Sullivan-Stewart. Her roommates said that she never came home from work last night. The news anchor didn't report her cause of death. All she said was that Lauraine's dead body was found in the ocean near the pier and that an autopsy was underway.

After a quick commercial break, the news anchor continued the story, bringing up the startling similarities between Lauraine and the other two victims: Patrice Dason and Kendra Puller. Patrice was the girl who died the day Mom and I moved in.

The footage on the TV changed to the beach, with the pier in the background. A reporter interviewed some witnesses who all said that a shark was to blame. But then the reporter made sure to point out that an official cause of death had yet to be determined and that no beach advisory had been issued.

I wondered if the only reason they weren't reporting a serial killer was on the loose was because the cops hadn't told them yet. Keeping this information a secret was probably crucial to their investigation. They probably didn't want anyone to know, for fear that they might tip off the killer, who they probably had already profiled and were in the process of tracking down, at least I hoped.

"So what's your opinion about all of this?" Hunter asked. "Do you think a shark killed those girls?"

"No, I don't. I think someone murdered them."

Hunter cocked his head. "But one of those people they interviewed said there was a shark tooth stuck in the body."

"Yeah, I know, but maybe it didn't get there on its own. I think a person is to blame."

"You do?"

"I've seen a lot of true crime documentaries. A serial killer usually leaves a calling card. Maybe the killer put the tooth there."

"That's possible, I guess." Hunter leaned forward, elbows on his knees. "Whatever killed those girls, if it was a shark or a person, I'd recommend that you just stay out of the ocean. It's better to be safe than sorry. I wouldn't want anything to happen to you." He reached down for Max's harness. "I'm gonna get going. Nevin and I are heading to the store soon."

I walked Hunter to the back door, and once he got outside, he said he could manage on his own from there. Just before he walked through the gate he turned back around. "Oh, yeah. I meant to ask you... Did you find that mystery item your aunt was supposed to have buried?"

"Nope. I didn't find anything."

"You should keep looking. You never know, it might just pop up randomly in a place you least expect."

I wasn't going to give up. Whatever she was supposed to bury, if I were to find it, it might help give me a clue as to what was going on. Finding out what happened to Aunt Emma was still a huge priority.

After I shut the back door, I laid down on the couch and fell asleep. I woke up an hour later to the sound of plastic sacks rattling in the kitchen. Mom was unpacking groceries. She was wearing a new outfit: a fitted skirt, a flower-patterned shirt, and a pearl necklace that I hoped was fake.

It surprised me that she had returned home so soon. Mom had a long history of disappearing for days at a time. I had hoped this habit of hers would stop now that we lived in this beautiful home, and maybe it had. Maybe she really did go help a friend who had car trouble and returned home after she had finished, like her note said.

In the past, whenever Mom would disappear, I always suspected that she did this because she was using drugs. But I couldn't prove it. I never found any narcotics stashed away, despite my many searches.

I accepted this part of Mom, the unreliable, unpredictable part, and rationalized in my mind that she just didn't know better, because she never had a proper role model to learn from.

She and Aunt Emma had been shipped around to several

different foster homes growing up. They were eventually split up when Mom went to juvenile detention for stealing money from a couple she was babysitting for. About a month after Mom got out of juvy, she stole again and got caught. This time she stole from her boyfriend's parents. Mom admitted to me that there had been numerous other times she stole from stores and random people, but she just hadn't gotten caught.

"Did you get my note?" Mom asked as she pulled a loaf of bread out of a grocery sack.

"Yes, I got it… I also got locked out of the house last night."

"You did? What happened?" She began moving grocery items from the counter to the refrigerator.

"I was locked outside for hours. Then Tim finally let me in after he took a marathon shower. I guess it takes a lot of shampoo and conditioner with all that hair of his."

"Hmm." Her forehead wrinkled, making her outfit look too young for her. "Who locked the door?"

"I thought you did."

"Me?" she grimaced. "You know I don't lock doors." She tossed a bag of chips on top of the refrigerator.

If Mom didn't lock me out, and Tim didn't either, then it must have been Tamara who locked me out.

"I'm going to make mac and cheese. Do you want some?" Mom held up the box.

"Sure. I'll have some."

Just then a new thought entered my mind. What if Tamara

wasn't trying to steal the letter from my purse? What if she put it in there? Did she write that letter to lure me out of the house? Why would she do that?

My mind continued to hover over this question.

The only thing I knew for sure was that somebody wrote that letter with manipulation in mind. Whether it was intended for Aunt Emma or me, I had no idea.

Either Tamara had put the letter in my purse, or she had tried to steal it from my purse. Or she had no idea the letter existed.

Mom turned the radio on to an eighties station and asked me if I would come stir the pasta. As soon as I picked up the spoon, the song playing on the radio ended and the news highlights of the day were announced. The dead girl from the pier was the top story. I listened intently, but there was no new information, no cause of death mentioned, no warnings about a serial killer or a killer shark.

I watched the water in the pot boil, the noodles churning, wondering when the serial killer would strike again.

CHAPTER 22

WINTER

Before eating dinner, I went upstairs to see if Tamara was home, just out of curiosity. Her bedroom door was locked. I knocked, but she didn't answer. Maybe she had left while I was asleep.

Then I checked to see if Tim was home, because Mom wanted me to ask him if he wanted to join us for dinner. His door was also locked, no answer. Maybe he was still at work.

I went back downstairs, and while Mom and I sat at the table together, I told her about everything that had happened while she was gone. I didn't hold any information back. She sat there listening to me, eating her mac and cheese, her eyes wide with surprise.

After I finished talking, she set down her fork and wiped her mouth. "You think Tamara is involved in Aunt Emma's death?"

"What other explanation is there? I caught her with her hand in my purse."

"Maybe that letter was part of a game. Maybe Emma was participating in a scavenger hunt, kind of like how people take part in murder mystery dinners."

I got up from my chair to go get the letter. I pulled out the book, opened it up, and the letter was gone. That's when I freaked out. I went through all of the books on the shelf, flipping through the pages, shaking them, looking behind the bookshelf, looking everywhere, but I couldn't find it.

Mom sat there watching me, eating her dinner, like this was just any other normal night of the week. When I finally calmed down enough to sit at the table again, Mom said, "In case you're wondering, I did not take the letter."

"I know you didn't," I snapped.

"Just wanted to make sure," Mom said as she shook some pepper on her mac and cheese.

"At least we know that letter was real and not part of a scavenger hunt," I said.

Mom let out a heavy sigh, wiping a napkin across her mouth. "Do you want me to talk to Tamara and see what I can find out? Will that make you happy?"

"You're kidding, right? You don't actually think she's going to tell you the truth, do you? This isn't mail theft or something stupid like that. This is murder."

Mom tossed her fork into her bowl, picked it up and took it to the sink. "I've got homework to do."

"Do not ask Tamara about this, Mom," I called as she walked away. "Don't mention anything about this to her."

"Okay," Mom groaned from the other end of the hall.

All I wanted was for her to believe me and actually give a care. Was that asking too much?

I really needed somebody to talk to, and the only person who came to my mind was Eli. It was getting late, so I figured he should be done with his lifeguard shift soon.

I slipped on my flip-flops and headed out to the beach. My timing couldn't have been more perfect. Jaxson had just left and Eli was about to head to his car.

He invited me to come up and sit on the tower with him. I told him about Aunt Emma and how I thought she had been murdered. I told him about the note and my suspicions surrounding Tamara.

"I don't know if you're aware of this," he said. "I knew Reginald. He would stop by and talk to me and Jaxson once in a while. But I never talked to your aunt. She seemed kind of shy. I would see her in your backyard sometimes. Did you know that she and Tamara were friends?"

I felt like I had just been knocked over by a big wave and was struggling to figure out which way was up. *Tamara was friends with Aunt Emma*, I repeated over and over in my mind, feeling numb. I figured they knew each other, but I didn't think they were close enough to be considered friends.

"I saw them hanging out together in your backyard several times." Eli turned and looked over his shoulder.

I also turned to look. While sitting on top of the tower, the view of my backyard was unobstructed.

"Tamara lied to me. She said she didn't know my aunt."

Eli stroked his chin, deep in thought, watching the seagulls fly around in front of us. Then his eyes slid over to me. "Do you have a lock on your bedroom door?"

"Yeah."

"Make sure you use it."

I chuckled, not because I thought what he said was funny, but because I was nervous. She wouldn't hurt me, would she?

"If things get really bad, you could always move in with me."

I knew Eli wasn't being serious, but still, the fact that he said this almost took my breath away. "You still live at home with your parents, right?" I smiled.

He shook his head. "I moved out. I have my own apartment."

"But aren't you still in high school?"

"Yeah. My dad got a job offer in Texas and I didn't want to move with my parents since I was going to be starting my senior year this fall. They were fine with me staying here, as long as I lived with my older brother, Nevin."

My stomach dipped. Was he just teasing me again? That couldn't be true. "Nevin's your brother?"

"Yeah. I thought you knew that."

"No, I had no idea." I squinted my eyes, staring at Eli, trying to match his features to Nevin's, but the puzzle pieces just wouldn't fit. Their bodies were both built and strong, but nothing else matched. Nevin had thin, straight red hair.

Eli had dark brown curls. Nevin's eyes were small, beady and shifty. Eli's were normal-sized, warm and inviting. "You look nothing alike."

"I know. We hear that a lot. I take after my dad. Nevin looks like our mom's side of the family."

"So, do you and Nevin get along?" I asked.

Eli stared out at the horizon, a breeze blowing through his curls. "It's not easy living with him. Nevin has a hard time telling the truth. He always has. I'm in the process of looking for a new place to live."

An older man who was walking by called to Eli, interrupting us. He started telling him about his latest fishing expedition. I sat there only half listening, my mind still spinning.

Why would Hunter have so much disdain for Eli, but place so much trust in his brother Nevin? And why was it so important to Hunter that I stay away from Eli? I wondered if Hunter was truly trying to protect me, or if this was his way of eliminating competition. Maybe Hunter liked me.

The man talking to Eli moved on, leaving us alone again.

"Something has been bothering me Eli," I said. "I don't understand this big grudge Hunter has against you.

Eli nodded slowly, biting his lip. He took a deep breath. "What did he tell you? Or did Nevin say something?"

Nevin had never mentioned Eli, but this response made me think. Maybe the problem was really between Eli and his brother. Hunter might have just been repeating what he heard from Nevin. That would explain why he didn't offer any details.

"It was Hunter. He told me I should stay away from you. He thinks you're dangerous, but he didn't explain."

"He told you I'm dangerous? Wow."

Eli's phone went off. He silenced it, then slid it back into the pocket of his shorts. "Sorry, Winter. I've got a second job that I need to get to. I'm a stocker over at Bert's Grocery."

"Oh. Okay. Well, I don't want to make you late." I had already monopolized way too much of his time today. I quickly climbed down the ladder. Eli and I walked together through my backyard, then he exited through the side gate and walked across the street to his car.

From the corner of my eye, I saw movement in Hunter's backyard. I stopped and turned to look, wondering if it was Hunter. But it wasn't. It was Nevin. He was standing there staring at me. Max darted past him, heading back into Hunter's house. Nevin gave me a forced smile, but I didn't smile back at him. I wanted so badly to go over there and tell him off. How could he betray his brother and tell lies about him?

Nevin turned and followed Max into Hunter's house.

The first thing I did when I went back inside my house was check to see if Tamara was home, but she wasn't. I laid down on the couch watching TV, listening for the front door. A couple hours had passed, and still no Tamara.

Since it was late, I decided I was going to have to confront her tomorrow about how she lied and said that she didn't know Aunt Emma, when in fact she did. I had proof. I had Eli as a witness.

Upstairs in my bathroom, I sat on the edge of the tub as the water warmed. I looked up at the window, and lightning flashed across the black sky.

I was in the shower, lathering shampoo in my hair, when thunder boomed, shaking the house. The lights in the bathroom flicked off, then on again. I quickly pumped some conditioner into the palm of my hand. The lights flickered again, so I moved even faster. Less than a minute later, I was out of the shower. A loud clap of thunder exploded, making me jump, and at the same time everything went dark. The power was out.

Unable to see anything, I felt my way along the bathroom wall, tripped over what I thought were my shoes, bumped my head on the open door, and finally found my towel.

There I was, stumbling around in the dark from a stupid power outage, while Hunter's entire world was like this every day. I didn't know how he managed to have such a positive attitude. He hadn't complained to me once.

Rain beat against the house, thunder rumbled. I wondered how much longer the power would be out. I didn't have a flashlight in here or a candle.

I wrapped my hair up in a towel and finished drying off.

After feeling my way along the wall through my bedroom, I arrived at my dresser. I had no idea what clothes I was selecting, but I managed to get a pair of shorts on and a shirt. As I closed the dresser drawer, I heard my bedroom door click shut, and a shudder of fear ripped through me as quick as lightning. Had someone just come in here, or did they just leave?

"Who's there?" I demanded, staring into the darkness.

Nobody responded.

Was it Tamara, I wondered. Was she in here? But why? She wouldn't do anything to hurt me, would she?

I moved slowly around my bed, trying not to make a sound, but my breathing was fast, much louder than I wanted it to be. I finally made it to the baseball bat that laid propped up against the wall. My fingers fumbled to grab hold of it, and I accidentally knocked it over. The metal handle skidded along the wall, then the bat landed with a crash and started rolling across the floor. I had no idea where it went, and I still didn't know if I was alone. I wanted something to protect myself with. I started feeling along the nightstand. Then the door creaked open and a faint beam of light cut through the darkness. My eyes strained to see who it was.

"Winter?" Mom called and relief swept through me.

I grabbed the flashlight from her hand. "I need this."

"What's the matter?"

"I heard a noise."

I searched through my bathroom and my closet. Nobody was there. I turned back to Mom. "Where's Tamara? Is she home?"

"I'm not sure who's home."

"Well, somebody was just in here. It had to have been Tamara or Tim."

Mom and I went upstairs to Tamara's room first. I pounded on the door. She didn't answer, and it was locked. She still could've been somewhere else in the house, and that made me nervous. Just how dangerous was she? But then again, maybe she hadn't been in my room at all. Maybe she wasn't even home.

The only other possibility was Tim. I sure hoped he wasn't a pervert or something worse.

We went to his room next. Mom nudged me out of the way and knocked on his door. "Tim, are you in there? Tim?"

A loud thud. It sounded like he tripped and fell. The door swung open. "Did we lose power?" he asked, squinting from the brightness of mom's flashlight. He seemed groggy, like he had just woken up.

"Yes, we did," Mom replied, lowering the light from his face.

"All right. I'll get dressed and come downstairs to start a fire."

Mom quickly turned around when she realized that Tim was only wearing boxer shorts. "Oh, okay… Thanks."

It didn't bother me that he wasn't dressed. He obviously wasn't embarrassed, otherwise he wouldn't have opened the door in his underwear. He would have covered up.

"Do you mind if I borrow your flashlight?" he asked.

Mom handed it to him from over her shoulder. She pulled me close and leaned into my ear. "I don't think he was in your room."

"Well, somebody was. The door didn't just shut on its own, and I had locked it."

Tim joined us in the hallway and handed Mom her flashlight. He had located a flashlight of his own. It was much bigger and brighter.

We made our way downstairs and found Tamara sitting in the family room. The light from her phone shined on her face with an eerie glow, sending a shiver through me. She was talking with someone and barely acknowledged us when we came in.

I felt certain that she was the one who had been in my room, only I couldn't prove it. All I had was an uneasy feeling that I just couldn't shake. Something wasn't right. I could sense the evil radiating from her, which I had originally chalked up to being an air of confidence. But there was so much more going on with her than that. I had felt this same kind of sensation before from Chaz, so I knew I wasn't imagining it.

Tamara lied about knowing Aunt Emma, and she had to have a good reason for that. What was she trying to hide? I wanted to confront her, but Mom needed my help collecting candles. We went from room to room, collecting as many as we could find, while Tim worked on building a fire in the fireplace. Tamara kept talking on her phone and didn't bother to help. No shock there.

Before long, the fireplace lit up the family room. Tim also brought in another flashlight from his truck and gave it to Mom since hers didn't work that well. I gladly took Mom's flashlight since I didn't have anything.

The doorbell rang.

"He's here," Tamara announced. "Gotta go." She lowered her phone, using it as a flashlight as she walked out of the room, high heels striking against the floor.

After the door slammed, I headed to the living room window and pushed the curtain aside. A tall truck sat parked in the driveway. When Tamara opened the door, the truck's interior lights didn't come on so I couldn't see who was driving.

The truck pulled out into the road, headlights flashing in my eyes. When I could see again, I spotted someone standing directly across the street next to the neighbor's garbage cans. But it was too dark to see their face. After the truck drove off, the street became pitch black, and I couldn't see the person standing there anymore. Through the crack in the curtain, I continued to keep watch.

Another car approached on the road. When its lights were close enough, I saw that same person again. I figured it was a man out there, based on how he was standing. His feet were spread wide apart. I continued to wait and watch, hoping that by the time the next car drove by, he would be gone.

As the long seconds ticked by, I became more concerned. Something wasn't right. It made no sense for that guy to be standing out there in the dark, in the rain, during a thunderstorm.

Suddenly a small beam of light appeared. It slowly moved across the street toward my house, then flashed up, pointing directly at me. I ducked down, watching the light move to the next window.

I crawled away, then ran back to the family room. "Someone's out front shining their flashlight in our windows. What if they're trying to break in?"

Tim moved past me, rushing toward the door. Mom and I watched as he ran out into the middle of the street. I shined my flashlight over at the garbage cans, but nobody was there. Soon Tim disappeared in the dark, and Mom and I just stood there waiting inside the house with the front door wide open.

"Do you think Tim needs our help?" I asked. "Maybe we should go out there and look for him."

Mom narrowed her eyes in disapproval. "He can manage on his own, I'm sure."

When Tim finally came back, he was soaking wet from the rain. His white T-shirt clung to his skin and was now see-through. "Whoever it was, they're long gone now. I chased him all the way to the end of the road." He wiped his face with the bottom of his drenched T-shirt.

Mom smiled at him, admiringly. "Thank you so much, Tim."

"Were you able to see who it was?" I asked.

Tim ran his fingers through his drenched mullet. "I only saw the back of him."

"So it was a guy, not a girl, right?"

He shrugged. "I actually don't know."

Come on. Give me something more than that. "Was the person taller than you?" Tim was probably about five foot ten.

He scratched the side of his face, contemplating my question. "I didn't get close enough to figure that out."

"Did you see their hair color?" I asked. "Was it long or short?"

He made a face, thinking.

I wanted to yell at him to hurry up and answer me. Why wasn't he trying harder to describe what he saw? He had a flashlight. He had to have seen something.

"Winter." Mom glared at me. "It was too dark outside for Tim to see. Just drop it. Whoever was out there, they're long gone now. Problem solved. Tim chased them away, so let's just be grateful."

"I am grateful," I gasped. How could she not realize that? "I'm just concerned he might come back. For all we know, he might be the serial killer who killed those girls."

Tim leaned back against the wall, smirking at me as though he was about to laugh. "A serial killer?"

"Yes." *I'm not delusional*, I wanted to say. *So quit looking at me like I am.*

Mom chuckled like she was embarrassed. "She's just talking about those shark attack victims. She thinks someone killed them."

"Oh, right." He nodded, the smile still on his face. "I think I heard about that. Wasn't there another body found today?"

The memory flashed through my mind: the girl's long hair, her pink dress, the lifeguard vomiting. "I was there when her body was discovered."

Tim's eyebrows shot up, forehead wrinkled. "No kidding. You were there?" He chuckled, but he wasn't laughing at me. He genuinely seemed surprised. "Well, that must've been an experience. I bet you're gonna have a few sleepless nights, probably some vivid nightmares. I get it now." He nodded, looking at Mom. "She got spooked. It's probably going to take a while to recover from that."

Mom's mouth gaped open. She was no longer embarrassed of me, nope, she was embarrassed about how she had acted. Mom placed her arm around my shoulder like she was a caring and nurturing mother. I knew this was all for Tim's benefit, not mine.

Tim asked me some questions about what happened at the pier today. I told him about the old man snagging the girl's body on his fishing line and how the entire area had been closed off.

"Didn't someone tell you that there was a shark tooth?" Mom asked, trying to contribute to the conversation. But I was going to get to that part. I hadn't forgotten.

"Sounds fishy to me—no pun intended," Tim said with a serious look on his face. "Even with a shark tooth left behind, none of this makes sense. I've lived at three different beaches, in three different states: Hawaii, California, and here in

North Carolina. And I have never heard of a shark attack victim being washed to shore, already dead."

"Is that right?" Mom asked, hanging on his every word. I was getting tired of her act. She needed to stop pretending to be someone she wasn't. Tim would realize eventually that she was selfish and far from being a concerned parent. I slipped out from under her arm and headed back to the family room.

The fire was putting off too much heat but we still needed it for light. I closed the curtain over the sliding glass door, first checking to make sure it was locked.

I slept in the family room on the couch with Mom. Tim slept on the recliner about two feet away from us, because Mom asked him to. I woke up several times that night thinking that I had heard a noise, but then the sound disappeared and I would doze back off to sleep again.

The power came back on sometime in the middle of the night, and in the morning the skies cleared.

While Mom was making pancakes for the three of us, I heard the front door creak open.

I quickly headed to the living room and saw Tamara climbing the stairs. She was carrying her high heels, walking with bare feet, and was wearing a more casual outfit than the one she had on last night.

I almost called out to her, but then I realized she was crying. I could hear her sobbing, and it was getting louder. Her head was hanging down, and she sounded truly distraught.

As much as I didn't want to have to put this conversation off, it seemed like it would be better to wait until later, after she finished crying about whatever had upset her. It couldn't have been anything that bad. She probably broke a nail or found out the guy she had gone out with last night was actually poor.

CHAPTER 23

TAMARA (BELLANY)

The money I stole from Roy's grandma had come in handy. I was able to pay for a boob job, a nose job, and cheek implants. I was wearing brown contact lenses and dyeing my hair blond. There was no way anyone from my past would recognize me now.

I returned to North Carolina for two reasons. One, my money supply was running low. And two, I had found a new source of income. Her name was Emma Covington. When I saw the huge rock on her finger, I knew right away she would be my next target.

Emma and I had sat next to each other while getting pedicures in New York. She was there on vacation. It didn't take long for me to weave myself into Emma's life. She was lonely. Her fiancé worked all the time, and he was never home.

Emma was a bit clingy and needy, basically annoying.

I could totally understand how it would be hard for her to make friends. Personally, I could barely tolerate her. Plus when people saw Emma with Reginald, they immediately labeled her as a gold digger, because of their huge age gap. None of Reginald's friends liked her, and neither did his family. So the situation was perfect for me.

My first priority was to take out Reginald, but as luck would have it, the old guy ended up dying on his own from a heart attack.

I thought Emma would be absolutely devastated over losing him, but the funny thing was, she didn't seem all that upset. She eventually admitted to me that she didn't love him. She just loved his money. Well, we both had that in common. And I also loved that five-carat diamond engagement ring he had given her.

When I arrived home this morning, I was wearing it on my finger. Luckily it was the finger on my right hand. If it had been on my left, Winter would have seen it.

She had come tearing into the living room so quickly, her feet all heavy and stomping, I knew she was mad about something. She had probably found out that the letter was missing from the book and was going to blame me.

I knew from experience that sometimes avoiding conflict required a little dramatic performance. So I started to cry. I could see Winter from the corner of my eye as I climbed the stairs. She was standing there, staring up at me with a scowl on her face. Didn't she know how ugly that made her look? Not flattering at all.

Nighty-night, I thought to myself. Me and my diamond ring are going to bed. I'll deal with you later.

CHAPTER 24

WINTER

During breakfast, Tim told us that he used to own a successful construction company several years ago called Shark Construction.

"Shark? Why did you call it that?" I asked.

Tim smiled proudly. "Because it's memorable. A perfect name for a construction company located at the beach."

I caught sight of his shark tattoo peeking out from under his sleeve when he reached across the table for the syrup. His tattoo was also memorable: a shark chomping down on a woman with drops of blood squirting out. It was morbid and disturbing.

Tim poured the syrup onto his pancake, then licked his finger way too loudly. He continued talking about his company and how he had landed huge contracts, made lots of connections in the community. Business was booming. He said he used to live in a house just like ours.

"So what happened to your company?" Mom asked.

Tim stabbed his fork into his pancake, making a sour face. "I went bankrupt, because people are sue happy and incompetent." He stirred his pancake around in a puddle of syrup. "My administrative assistant let my company's insurance policy lapse. Then somebody got injured on one of my jobsites. I got sued and lost everything, even my wife. She didn't want to be with someone who was broke and a failure."

"You're not a failure," Mom said. "It wasn't your fault the insurance policy lapsed."

If Tim lost everything, then the injury must have been really bad. Or maybe Tim just had a terrible lawyer. "Did someone die?"

Tim shook his head, rolling his eyes. "Nobody died." He stuffed another bite of pancake into his mouth.

"Did they become crippled or disabled?" I asked.

He shrugged. "You know how it is, people like to play the victim."

Was he deliberately trying to avoid answering my question? "What happened? Who got injured? How bad was it?"

Mom sighed. "Winter," she said, disapprovingly. "You're being a bit nosy."

"I'm just curious. It's not a secret is it, Tim?" I asked him this on purpose, hoping to put him on the spot and make him feel uncomfortable. He was the one who brought this up in the first place, probably so he could impress Mom. He needed to explain himself.

"No, of course not. It's not a secret." He set his fork down, lacing his fingers together on the table. He motioned with his head. "The boy next door."

"Hunter?"

Tim nodded, eyebrows raised. "Yep. He's the one who got injured."

"What?" I gasped, absolutely stunned.

Then I remembered what Hunter had said to me. He said that I shouldn't trust Tim and that Tim did shoddy construction work. He said that Tim might try to swindle Mom and me out of rent money. All the pieces fell into place and now it was perfectly clear. Hunter had said those things because of what he went through, because of the accident that caused him to lose his eyesight. He must absolutely hate Tim.

"One of my employees was doing some remodeling at Hunter's family's house," Tim explained. "My employee hadn't finished installing the railing on the second story. He was still in the process of securing it, but then Hunter came along and he tripped or something. I don't know what happened, but he landed on the railing, and it just snapped. Then Hunter fell. He sustained a severe head injury which resulted in a condition called cortical blindness. Hunter's blindness was one of the rare cases that never improved. His family sued me and won."

I couldn't believe what I had just heard. I had been wondering how Hunter lost his sight ever since I met him, and now I knew.

What I didn't understand was why Hunter would move back to a place that held such bad memories? I sure wouldn't.

Then I realized that another one of my questions about Hunter had been answered. Now I knew how he could afford to live in that house.

It seemed strange that Tim would want to live next door to Hunter. Wouldn't seeing Hunter and the house he lived in serve as a constant reminder to Tim of painful memories from the past? Maybe it was possible that he didn't know Hunter lived next door until after he moved in. But if I were Tim, I would have moved out by now and found another place to live.

We continued to eat in silence, until Mom finally spoke up and changed the subject. She started talking about college and how she felt out of place there because the other students in her classes were so much younger than her. She also talked about how difficult her classes were. "I'm wondering if I need to get a tutor," she said.

Tim grinned. "I would offer to help you with your homework, but I wouldn't want you to fail."

Mom laughed a little too loudly at his joke. I didn't think it was that funny.

Tim drank the last of his milk and wiped his mouth with the back of his hand instead of his napkin. "Thanks for making breakfast again. This was really delicious." He looked at me. "Your mother is a great cook."

I couldn't make sense of Tim's comment. All Mom knew

how to cook was food that came in a box and only required three ingredients or less.

Tim stuffed his last bite of pancake into his mouth. "You know what I really hate about having lost my company? Seeing where all my money went."

"What do you mean?" Mom asked.

"I mean seeing how the people who sued me are living off it, as if they earned it and didn't steal it away from me." He pointed his fork at his chest. "It just gets me right here in the heart."

Did Tim think that he was the victim and that Hunter wasn't? This was not a good sign. He was beginning to remind me of every single one of Mom's past boyfriends. They all acted like they were entitled, that they had been wronged by someone, and they were the victims of an unjust society. Nothing was ever their fault.

After Tim headed off to work, Mom decided she better go upstairs and do some homework, even though she "didn't feel like it." But before she left the kitchen, she brought up the subject of Tamara, wondering where she had been all night, speculating that maybe she had a boyfriend.

"I sure hope so," I replied. "Maybe she'll move in with him instead of living here with us."

I spent most of my morning going through Aunt Emma's bedroom, hoping I would find a journal, maybe some pictures, or anything that would help me find out what was going on in her life before she died. Mostly, I wanted to find some kind of proof that she had been friends with Tamara.

After I had searched through every drawer, box, cupboard, shelf, and piece of paper, I still had zero evidence to prove that Tamara was somehow involved in Aunt Emma's life.

I sat on the bed, feeling frustrated. There wasn't anything personal in this bedroom except for the picture of Aunt Emma and Reginald. Someone had gone through her stuff and gotten rid of all of it.

I picked up the picture, and then I saw something that I hadn't noticed before. There was an engagement ring on Aunt Emma's finger. Her hand was angled and in a shadow, so I could only see part of it, but the diamond looked huge.

I scanned the room looking for a jewelry box. It seemed strange that she didn't have one. I checked the bathroom, the closet, every possible place she might have kept her ring. Maybe it fell off her finger. I checked under the cushions on the recliners, under the bedspread, under the mattress, under the bed—I crawled around her entire bedroom looking for it, but it was nowhere.

I went to Mom's bedroom and explained everything to her, including how Eli had seen Tamara talking to Aunt Emma in the backyard several times. Mom set down her laptop and called Mr. Davis. She put her phone on speaker so I could listen in.

His secretary answered and put Mom through to Mr. Davis, after five minutes of being on hold. He said he wasn't aware of an engagement ring. It hadn't been included on her list of assets. Mom asked if we could get a copy of Aunt

Emma's bank statements since we never got those. He said he would look into it and get back to her. But it sure seemed like he just wanted to get off the phone and wasn't interested in helping us.

Mom and I went back to Aunt Emma's bedroom to search for the engagement ring again. We checked and rechecked. We looked everywhere. Nothing. It was missing. But was it lost or stolen?

Mom picked up the picture from the nightstand. "That diamond looks like it's at least five carats—I don't know. Maybe it's bigger than that. It's hard to tell." Mom held out her hand, probably envisioning how Aunt Emma's ring would look on her finger.

"I think I know what happened," I said. "Tamara wrote that threatening letter. And she wrote others like it too. The previous letters probably threatened Aunt Emma that if she didn't bury her diamond engagement ring under the lifeguard tower, then she was gonna be killed."

Mom bit her lip, thinking. "If she finds out that we know what she's done..." Mom looked down, slumping her shoulders. "I thought everything was going to be so easy here, but it's not. I'm sorry I didn't take that letter seriously. Do you think Tamara's dangerous? Are we in danger?"

Probably, but I wasn't going to say that out loud. "There's two of us, and one of her. Plus we have Tim on our side. She can't do anything to us."

Mom seemed to be a little more hopeful after we talked

some more. She went back to her bedroom to do her homework, and I went downstairs to make myself something to eat. I was surprised, honestly, at how much better I was handling the situation compared to Mom. I didn't feel sad or scared anymore. I just had a determination inside me, a fire that I couldn't suppress. I was going to figure out a way to expose Tamara's lies.

I laid two pieces of bread out on a plate, then grabbed the jar of peanut butter. I dipped the dull knife in the jar, pulled it out, and the knife just about dropped from my hand when Tamara walked into the kitchen.

She was listening to music through her earbuds. I wanted so badly to pull a sharp knife out of the drawer and threaten her with it; demand that she tell me what happened to Aunt Emma. I wanted to know the truth, and I wanted her to pay for what she had done. But I knew I couldn't threaten her with a deadly weapon. That wouldn't get me anywhere, except for jail. Somehow I was going to have to calm myself down and coexist with her. I would have to tolerate her presence in this house until I could prove that she was somehow involved in Aunt Emma's death.

"Hold on," Tamara said, yanking her earbuds out. She pointed to the mound of peanut butter globbed onto the dull knife in my hand. "Don't make that crappy sandwich. I'll buy you lunch instead." She started counting on her fingers as she spoke. "I'll pay for your gas, buy your lunch, just take me to the store first—"

My fingers squeezed the handle of the knife. Tamara was lucky this thing wasn't sharp. "I can't take you right now." I started spreading the peanut butter onto my slice of bread, trying to calm down.

"We can go somewhere better for lunch this time. We don't have to go get burgers and fries. How does shrimp sound?" She kept talking. She kept suggesting different restaurants, asking what kind of food I liked, giving me her recommendations. She wouldn't shut up.

Why would she rent a bedroom from us? What was she up to? Was she living here so she could get rid of that letter and any evidence that might connect her to the crimes she had committed? Was she the one who went through Aunt Emma's things and got rid of all her personal items? Was she just that sick and twisted in her head, that the memories of what she had done to Aunt Emma didn't faze her?

"Winter?" Tamara's voice penetrated my thoughts. "Did you not hear me?"

My entire body tensed. I couldn't do this. I couldn't pretend like Tamara hadn't possibly murdered Aunt Emma. Just the mere sound of her voice was grating on my nerves. I spun around, glaring at her. My gaze shifted down to her hand. I wondered if she had tried on Aunt Emma's engagement ring before she sold it, or maybe she still had it hidden away somewhere.

The dull knife dropped from my grasp, crashing onto the tile floor. "Just shut up!" I snapped. "I don't want to eat lunch with you now or ever! I know you took that letter. I know you've been lying to me. You said you didn't know my aunt, but you did. Eli saw you with her. Why did you lie about knowing her? Is it because you killed her? Did you push her down the stairs? Did you kill her, so that you could steal from her? Where's my aunt's engagement ring?"

Tamara stared at me and didn't respond. I expected her to be frightened, or at least be surprised at my accusations, but her expression was stone cold. "I didn't do any of those things," she said, her words measured and deliberate. "How could you accuse me of murdering her and stealing from her? Maybe you should think about getting on some medication, because you sound like you're paranoid and delusional."

The rage inside me exploded, and the next thing I knew, I had Tamara pinned up against the wall, my fist cocked back.

She didn't look the slightest bit scared or intimidated—no, nothing like that. Her reaction took place in her eyes, which were normally sparkling and bright. But now they looked shallow and evil. She reminded me of Chaz. He had the very same haunting look in his eyes the night he murdered Venus and her siblings. Chaz didn't feel remorse or guilt for what he had done. He was a sociopath. I felt certain that Tamara was a sociopath too.

If I hit her, would she call the cops? Would she not react right now at all and take revenge on me later? Would she get back at me by doing something to Mom? I couldn't take that risk.

I let go of her shirt and stepped back. She turned and walked off at a normal, casual pace without saying another word to me.

As I stood there, still high on adrenaline, my thoughts shifted to Chaz again. He swore to me that he just wanted to talk to Venus. He said that she wasn't returning his calls or texts, and all he wanted to do was repair their relationship and work things out. He begged me to go with him to her house.

When I rang the doorbell, Venus came to the door, but she wouldn't open it and let us in. Chaz continued to act like the victim, manipulating me into feeling sorry for him. He actually started crying. So I used the spare house key that was hidden under a potted plant. I slid it into the lock, then both Chaz and I walked inside.

Venus was furious, of course. She was the one who started yelling at Chaz first. Then I saw a change come over him. He had those exact same unfeeling, evil eyes as Tamara. I tried to convince Chaz that we should leave, but he wouldn't listen, and I was getting worried. I wanted to call someone for help but didn't want to do it in front of him. So I offered to take Jess and Jonah upstairs. I told them to call their parents and explain that Chaz wouldn't leave. Their parents were just down the street at a neighbor's house and said they would come right away.

I left Jess and Jonah in the bonus room and walked down the hall to use the bathroom. My bladder felt like it was about to burst. I had drunk a humongous Diet Coke about an hour before I got there, and if I didn't make it to the bathroom soon, I was going to pee my pants. As soon as I was done using the bathroom, I was going to go back downstairs and tell Chaz that he better leave because Mr. and Mrs. Swensen would be there any minute.

I had just flushed the toilet when I heard a loud bang. I thought maybe the noise had come from the TV, only because I didn't want to believe the other possibility. When the second loud bang went off, I realized that Chaz had already come upstairs. I jumped inside the bathtub and hid behind the shower curtain. Another loud bang. I thought I was going to die that night. But Chaz never came for me.

The cops almost charged me with being his accomplice, for breaking and entering, and for a bunch of other crimes they had initially accused me of.

In spite of being two thousand miles away, the memories of that night felt closer than they had in months.

I looked down at the knife and the peanut butter on the floor. I was about to clean it up when someone knocked on the back door. It was Hunter.

"I've got a plumbing emergency," he said. "Nevin's working his other job today, and I could really use your help."

I followed him to his house. The pipes under the kitchen sink were leaking. Water was spewing everywhere. Hunter had already spread out towels on the floor. I found some bowls to help catch the water. I kept switching the bowls and dumping the water out when they got full until the plumber arrived.

When I walked back into my house, I was about to go upstairs and look for Mom, but she was in the living room, standing by the front door.

"Are you going to school?" I asked her.

She pointed over her shoulder. "No. Tamara just left. I was helping her with her luggage."

"Luggage? Where is she going?"

"She's going on vacation, heading down to Florida for the next couple weeks. She said she's going to go to Disney World and Universal with some friends. She seemed really excited about it."

That didn't sound right. I glanced up at the clock. "Mom, just about an hour ago, Tamara asked me to take her to the store. She was trying to bribe me with a free lunch and gas money. She didn't mention anything about going to Florida."

"Really?" Mom headed over to the window and looked outside. I opened the door. The car that had picked Tamara up was already gone.

"Mom."

She let go of the curtain, turning to face me. "What?"

"I kind of blew up at Tamara. I accused her of stealing Aunt Emma's engagement ring. I accused her of murdering her too."

Mom's mouth dropped open. She stared at me for a few

beats like she had just seen a ghost. "Now I know why she had all that luggage. I think she just moved out."

I grabbed the key to Tamara's bedroom out of Mom's purse and ran up the stairs with Mom trailing behind me. Tamara's bedroom door was unlocked. We stepped inside, confirming our worst fears. Everything was gone. She had moved out.

Mom immediately called the cops. An hour later, an officer named Randy Hansen came to the house. He asked if we knew what Tamara's previous address was, or if we had a copy of her driver's license. We didn't have any of that information. She had paid us in cash, so there wasn't a bank account with her name on it either. We didn't have a single shred of evidence to prove that Tamara even existed.

Officer Hansen said that he would be in touch, but I wasn't holding out much hope that his investigation would turn up anything. I doubted he would ever find her. Besides that, there was no way to prove that Tamara had stolen the engagement ring or that she murdered Aunt Emma. All Mom and I had were a bunch of accusations and zero proof.

Tim came home from work early to change all the locks on the doors, just in case Tamara came back. But I doubted she would ever show her face around here again. She had gotten the letter, and that was the last piece of evidence connecting her to Aunt Emma's murder.

I headed out to the beach so I could tell all of this to Eli. Jaxson was there, so he heard the story too.

"I knew it!" Jaxson jumped out of his chair, arms flailing. "I knew that girl was trouble! I told you she was, brah. I called it," he said, triumphantly. "I told you she lied about me. I never asked her out. I don't date trashy skanks." Jaxson's eyes suddenly got about two sizes bigger. "Cover for me," he said, climbing down the ladder.

"Where are you going?" Eli asked.

"I'm gonna dig for that diamond ring under this tower. If there's something there, I'll find it. I've done a lot of treasure hunting in my past. My brother used to bury my toys in our yard all the time when we were kids."

"I already looked," I said. "I dug a really deep hole. There wasn't anything there."

He cocked his head, a look of intrigue in his eyes. "It doesn't hurt to double-check."

I knew he wouldn't find anything, but he seemed determined.

"Go ahead," Eli said with a shrug. "I'll keep watch."

"Yes." Jaxson clapped his hands. "Treasure hunting time."

Eli wrapped his arms around me, catching me by surprise. "You look like you need a hug, Win."

He called me *Win*. Eli had given me a nickname, and it was much better than the one Jaxson had given me. Snow Queen. I melted into his arms, not wanting to let go.

"Still nothing!" Jaxson called from below. "But I'm gonna keep digging."

"I should have told you the real reason I was digging under

the tower that day," I confessed. "I obviously wasn't building a sandcastle."

"Don't worry about it," Eli said, letting go of me.

"Still nothing!" Jaxson called out.

"Do you need me to change the locks on your house?" he asked. "She still has a key, right?"

"Tim's taking care of that."

Eli turned his gaze to look out at the swimmers. "For the record, I'm not ignoring you," he said. "I've gotta keep watch."

"I know you do."

"Still nothing!" Jaxson called again.

A few minutes later, Jaxson finally decided to give up. The ring wasn't there.

The three of us continued to talk for a while and surprisingly Jaxson did not get on my nerves. I appreciated that he hated Tamara. Somehow that helped me feel better. And that hug Eli had given me, I was still thinking about how good it felt.

CHAPTER 25

WINTER

The next day, Tim came home from work early, and he didn't look good. I wondered if he was sick.

Mom noticed the distraught look on his face too. "Are you okay, Tim?"

He took a deep breath and just as he was about to say something, he stopped and turned his back to us.

Mom and I exchanged confused looks.

When he finally turned back around, a tear was rolling down his cheek. "My mother passed away," he said, his voice strained. Mom got up from the couch and wrapped him in a hug, trying to console him. She convinced him to sit down and tell us what happened.

His mother had been battling stomach cancer for the past year. Mom asked him if she could do anything for him. At first he said he didn't know, but then he started talking about making arrangements to fly back to Hawaii for the funeral.

Mom brought out her laptop so he could use it to purchase a plane ticket.

There was nothing I could do to help, so I went to the kitchen to clean. Then I went upstairs to do a load of laundry.

When I came back downstairs again, I overheard Mom and Tim discussing plans to go to Hawaii together.

"You're going with him?" I asked, surprised and confused. Why would she do that? Was he paying for her trip? Did she just want a free vacation? She had always said that she wanted to visit Hawaii one day.

Mom placed her hand on Tim's arm, rubbing it. That's when I noticed how close she was sitting next to him. Were they seeing each other?

"Tim wants me to go with him, and I think I should."

"Really?" I asked, still trying to register in my mind what was going on.

Tim's phone rang. "Hello," he said, getting up from the couch and heading down the hall.

Mom needed to think about this some more. She couldn't just drop everything and go. "What about school?"

"I'll be fine," she said dismissively. "I can miss a few days and still get caught up on my assignments."

I doubted that was the case. Mom was already struggling. "If you fall behind in your classes, it'll be really hard to catch up. Why are you dropping everything for Tim? Is there something going on between you two that I'm not aware of?"

Mom looked at me with sheepish eyes, and my stomach knotted up. I had seen that look many times before. "Tim and I have been seeing each other. Things are starting to get serious."

"What?" I gasped in disbelief. How could I have not noticed what was going on with them? I searched my memory, only to realize right away all the signs that I had missed. Mom would get up early in the morning and come downstairs for breakfast the same time Tim did, while I stayed in bed to sleep in. There had also been many nights when I had gone to bed and she and Tim stayed up together. "Were you deliberately hiding your relationship from me?"

"I knew you wouldn't approve. You would say that I was jumping into things too quickly."

"Well, you are."

"No. I'm not." Mom walked over to the table and started rummaging through her purse. So apparently her mind had been made up. The discussion was over. Lovely.

She pulled out some cash and handed it to me. "This is for groceries and gas while I'm gone."

I set the cash down on the table and followed her into the kitchen, wondering how I could convince her to stay. But how could college compete with Hawaii?

She grabbed a couple granola bars out of the cupboard and stuffed them into her purse. "I've got to go pack," she said, taking off down the hall.

I followed her up the stairs to her room.

She pulled out a suitcase and set it on the bed, then opened a dresser drawer and began searching through it, tossing socks and other random clothing items onto the floor. She pulled out a brand-new black bathing suit with the price tag still on it and set it inside the suitcase.

The distant look in her eyes told me she was already dreaming about Hawaii. Her mind had been made up. She was going, no matter what I said to her.

Mom held up two dresses in front of her as she looked at her reflection in the mirror. The dresses still had the price tags on them. I reached inside her suitcase, moving her clothes around, noticing a whole lot of price tags. All of this stuff was brand-new. How much money had she been spending on clothes? I hadn't checked the bank account in a couple weeks. Had she already drained it? Is that why she offered me cash, because that was all that was left?

Mom smiled at her reflection, holding up two more new dresses. "Maybe I'll just take all of them." She scanned the room. "Am I forgetting anything?"

Yeah, I wanted to say. You should probably wipe that smile off your face. Tim's mom died. You wouldn't want him to figure out too soon how selfish and self-centered you are.

I sat there watching her gleefully pack her suitcase, trying to stop myself from getting angry. She was being irresponsible.

"Oh, I know what I forgot." She grabbed her curling

iron from the bathroom and stuffed it into her overflowing suitcase.

My gaze swept across the bedroom, landing on the backpack that was sitting on the floor next to a pile of dirty clothes. I got up from the bed and went over to pick it up. "Don't forget about this."

Mom bit her lip, making a face like she was about to refuse a second helping of vegetables. "Thanks."

I carried the backpack full of her school things downstairs and set it next to her suitcase. She wandered around the house, making sure she hadn't forgotten anything. I still couldn't believe what was happening. I was going to be alone in this big house.

Mom checked her phone. "It's almost three o'clock, Tim," she called. "Sorry, honey. We've got to get on the road if we're going to catch this flight."

"I wish you weren't leaving," I said.

I walked outside with her and Tim. He loaded their luggage into his truck and we said our goodbyes. When Mom and I hugged, I held on to her much longer than I normally would.

She noticed the redness in my eyes after we let go and placed her hands on my shoulders. "You're going to be just fine. I know you will. And I know you're not going to miss me. You've got Eli to keep you company." Mom gave me one more quick hug. "Don't throw any parties while I'm gone," she chuckled.

"Have a safe trip."

I watched the truck drive down the road before heading back inside the house.

Mom's backpack was still sitting on the floor at the bottom of the stairs. I knew she had left it on purpose. I picked it up and stuffed it into the closet. Mom wasn't going to finish college.

I walked into the family room, then through the back door, heading for the beach.

When I arrived at the lifeguard tower, Eli looked down at me. "Come on up."

I sat next to him in Jaxson's usual spot, since he wasn't there. "What's wrong?" Eli asked.

Everything came flying out of my mouth; how Mom had taken off with Tim and was giving up on college; how she was throwing her life away for a man just like she had always done in the past. I even told him about Kyle, and how he had died, but I didn't tell him that I felt responsible. I didn't tell him about the blanket.

Then I told him about what happened with Chaz. I told him that I was the one who let Chaz into the house; how I used the spare house key, and then I hid in the bathtub while gunshots were going off.

Eli listened to everything. His eyes were mostly on the ocean watching the swimmers, but I didn't mind. I felt as though I was sitting in a confessional, baring my soul, and it felt so liberating. I wanted to tell Eli everything about Kyle, but I wasn't ready to come completely clean of all my secrets. I just wanted to make a start and begin the process of emotional healing. I felt like I could trust Eli and that he wouldn't judge me.

"Sorry for talking your ear off," I said, realizing I should probably shut up now.

He looked at me from the corner of his eye for a long moment. "If you think all of that stuff you told me is going to scare me off, you're wrong." He reached for my hand and looked directly at me. I felt like I was drowning in his eyes. I couldn't look away even if I wanted to. "I'll come over in a couple hours after my shift is over, but I can only stay for an hour before I have to go to my next job." He traced his thumb across the back of my hand. "I can come back over after work at midnight."

"That sounds good to me," I said, trying not to blush.

His eyes shifted, and I followed his gaze. An ATV was heading our direction. Jaxson was driving it.

I stood up. "I'll see you later."

Eli stepped in close to me. "Winter," he whispered. "I know this isn't the best timing with all that you have going on, but I can't let you go without doing this first." He reached out, brushing a strand of hair from my face, his fingers gliding along my cheek, leaving a trail of heat. His gaze lowered to my lips and my heart stopped. All I could think about was him. I felt like I had escaped from all of my fears and everything I had done wrong in my past—every bit of it was forgotten, just for that moment. His kiss was quick and gentle, yet powerful enough to make my knees weak. He was wrong about one thing: This was the best timing. I needed that more than he could ever know.

Eli watched me climb down the ladder. When my feet hit the sand, I turned around and my stomach dropped. Nevin was lying on a towel a couple feet away with his baseball cap covering his face. Had he been listening in on our conversation? Had he heard me spilling my guts?

Nevin's arm moved. He lifted the hat off his face. I swallowed hard, my throat feeling tight and dry. I guessed that answered my question. He wasn't asleep. He heard everything.

The ATV's engine grew louder, then finally cut off. Jaxson had his phone wedged between his shoulder and ear. He grinned at me, winked, then climbed up the ladder.

Nevin shifted up onto his elbows, his long body still sprawled out, feet crossed at the ankle. He smiled and my stomach continued to twist. He knows all about me now. He intentionally invaded my privacy.

"Winter," his voice carried through the air, along with the squawk of a passing seagull.

He stuck his baseball cap on top of his head before standing. My fingernails dug into the palms of my hands. He nodded toward the lifeguard tower, and I thought to myself, here it comes. He's going to say something about Kyle or about Chaz.

Nevin stared at me with his muddy brown eyes. "Want to go for a swim? You turned me down last time, remember? How about this time? Are you still afraid of sharks?"

I shook my head and started to walk away. Not only did I feel like my privacy had been violated, but I was still mad at Nevin for lying about Eli and accusing him of abuse when they were younger.

"Hey," Nevin said, appearing at my side. My feet stopped. I didn't want him coming with me to my house. I looked back at the lifeguard tower, but Eli and Jaxson were watching the water, not me.

"I wanted to talk to you."

Again, I glanced at the lifeguard tower. I wished that Eli would come over here. *Turn around and look*, I thought to myself as if he could hear my thoughts.

"Are you okay?" Nevin asked.

I narrowed my eyes. "What do you want?"

"I just wanted to explain to you what happened on the pier."

The pier? Was he talking about the dead girl?

"I wanted to clear some things up," Nevin said, holding his hands up in mock surrender. "Hunter told me what you said about that night at the pier, when Matt and I got into that fight. I wasn't trying to scare him just for the fun of it. I did it to protect you."

I shot him a look of confusion.

Nevin gestured toward the lifeguard tower. "I had Jaxson take Matt's shoes to stop him from following you."

"What?" I asked, wondering how this made any sense. "Why would he want to follow me?"

"Matt saw me talk to you, and when you walked past us

without stopping, he saw that as a challenge. He told me he was going to follow you. He saw that you were alone."

My eyes widened. Nevin sounded like he was telling me the truth, and it all made sense, especially since he told Jaxson to throw Matt's shoes into the ocean.

Nevin shook his head. "I wasn't going to let him near you. We took his car keys too. You can ask Jaxson if you don't believe me."

I wondered why Jaxson hadn't explained this to me already. Jaxson could have taken some of the credit for watching out for me, spun the story however he wanted. Did Jaxson actually have a humble side to him? Was that why he didn't tell me? And as for Nevin, why hadn't he told me this sooner? I tried to remember what Matt looked like, but I couldn't. All I remembered was that he had dark hair and was wearing blue shorts.

"Matt hasn't bothered you, has he?"

I thought about the guy with the flashlight who Tim chased away on the night of the thunderstorm. But how was I supposed to know if that was Matt? "I have never met Matt. I don't even know what he looks like."

"Well, maybe he learned his lesson then, since he hasn't bothered you."

"Do you think there's still a chance he could?"

"Nah, you should be fine. If he hasn't caused you any trouble, then you don't need to worry about him."

I hoped he was right about that, but how could he be sure? "Thanks for sticking up for me."

"Of course."

We stood there in silence for a few beats. This was awkward. "I'm going to head home. Thanks again."

"Hey, I was wondering if maybe you would like to go to dinner tonight? Or we could go tomorrow—whenever's convenient for you."

My mouth gaped open as I searched for the right words to say.

"Oh," he nodded, "you're seeing someone, aren't you." He smiled. "It's not Eli, is it?"

The wind blew my hair into my face. I pushed it back, gathering my thoughts before I replied. Nevin and Eli were brothers, and there was already a rift between them.

"I can't go to dinner with you. I have plans with Eli, and"

He held up his hand to stop me. "No need to explain. I get it." He forced a smile. "Guess I wasn't fast enough."

Actually, that wasn't it at all. He had to realize that, didn't he? He never had a chance with me. I pointed over my shoulder. "I'm gonna get going."

His forced smile turned into a frown. "See ya around."

As I walked through my backyard, I kept wondering why Nevin would ask me out after he had listened in on my conversation with Eli. He knew Eli was coming over later. Did Nevin think I would go out with him after Eli left? Even if Nevin hadn't heard my conversation with Eli, he still had to have seen me with him on top of the lifeguard tower.

CHAPTER 26

WINTER

When I went back inside the house, I was about to head upstairs to my bedroom, but then I saw the mail truck pass by the front of the house, so I decided to get the mail first.

As I shuffled through the stack of envelopes, I came across a piece of mail addressed to Hunter. With his letter in hand, I walked next door and rang the doorbell. He didn't answer, so I knocked. Still no answer. As I started back down the steps, I heard the door creak open behind me.

Hunter's black hair was flattened on one side. The buttons on his shirt were undone, exposing his smooth chest.

"Hey, Hunter. I brought over a letter that was delivered to my house by mistake."

He opened the door wider, exposing his right arm. It was wrapped in a bandage from elbow to wrist, a spot of blood seeping through about midway down his arm.

"What happened to your arm?"

"A dog bite." He moved his arm and winced in pain. "I was trying to stop another dog from attacking Max." Just then Max appeared, sticking his nose out the door.

"Did Max get hurt?"

"The vet said he's fine."

"So how bad is it?"

"Twelve stitches." The corners of Hunter's mouth turned down slightly.

That sounded pretty bad, and the blood seeping through the bandage made it look painful. "Is it supposed to be bleeding like that?"

He dropped his head back in frustration. "It soaked through again?"

"I can help you change your bandage if you want." I wondered how bad his injuries would look. Hopefully it wasn't too gruesome.

"I'd appreciate that. Nevin has the day off."

I followed him through his house to the kitchen. This time his house didn't smell like bleach. "Where do you want me to put your mail?"

"You can set it on the desk."

My eyes searched around the kitchen and the adjoining family room for the desk he was referring to. Around the corner and next to the window sat a large oak desk with stacks of paper piled on top of it. "Is there a specific spot you want me to put it?"

"Just put it anywhere. I'll have Nevin take care of it when he comes tomorrow." Hunter retrieved a small basket of first aid supplies from the cupboard in the kitchen.

I sat down next to him at the table and began going through the contents of the basket. "I think everything's here, except I don't see any scissors."

Hunter slammed his fist on the table, which surprised me. I didn't expect him to get angry. "I can't believe he didn't put those back in there," he grumbled. "I'm going to have to call him. I have no idea where he put them." Hunter left the room with Max trailing behind.

I looked around the family room for the scissors but didn't find them. Since the kitchen was close by, I decided to look around there too.

The pantry door was wide open. Apparently Nevin was not a very good housekeeper. A spilled sack of potatoes laid on the floor next to my feet—a potential trip hazard for Hunter. I picked them up and moved them out of the way, then noticed a pile of laundry stuffed in the corner. This was Nevin's job but I wanted to be helpful, so I scooped up the clothes and started searching for the laundry room. I found it right away. It was down the hall from the kitchen.

I set the pile of clothes on the counter and began to separate them into piles of lights and darks. Two large white towels sat on top. As soon as I picked one up, I found a huge dark stain. It was saturated. The other towel had a stain on it too. Did Hunter really bleed that much from his dog bite? It was going to take a lot of bleach to clean these, and even then I wasn't sure if the stains would come out.

Next I picked up a shirt, and I dropped it immediately, my heart jumping into my throat. That little voice inside my head which usually warned me when something was wrong was screaming at me to run, but my feet wouldn't move. I felt almost certain that what I was looking at had been used to kill those three girls. Lying there on the counter, mixed in with the pile of clothes, was a single black glove. It had metal blades protruding from the fingertips, shaped like shark teeth, and they appeared to be covered in what looked like blood, mixed with sand or dirt.

I didn't know how long I had been standing there staring at that glove in abject fear. My mind barely registered the voice calling my name. I felt like I was stuck in a dream state, that I was on the verge of waking up but couldn't quite get there. I was unsure if what I was hearing was coming from the real world or if I was just imagining it.

"Winter," Hunter's husky voice called out much louder. This time I knew it was coming from somewhere in the house. This was real. Everything was real. The voice inside my head boomed, get out of here! Run!

I stepped out into the hall and peeked around the corner, my heart pounding wildly in my chest. I leaned forward to check and see if Hunter was there before I stepped into the kitchen and nearly leaped out of my flip-flops. He was standing in the kitchen with a pair of scissors in his hand, his back facing me.

"Winter," he called out again.

With nowhere else to go, I slipped back into the laundry room and hid behind the open door.

"Winter, where are you? Are you still here?"

I pressed my back against the wall, hoping the door would hide me. Footsteps approached. That was when I realized my mistake. I had left the glove lying on the counter in plain sight. Hunter would see it there. I knew he could see. He wasn't blind.

I abandoned my hiding spot, ran to the counter, scooped up the pile of clothes, and tossed them into one of the laundry baskets. Then I ran back behind the door, struggling to control my breathing, on the verge of panicking.

Hunter's footsteps grew louder, until I heard him enter the laundry room. I hoped he wouldn't notice the pile of clothes in the basket, but I didn't have time to find a better spot to hide them.

His feet moved across the floor, then suddenly stopped. I closed my mouth, trying to breathe quietly through my nose. Had he seen it, I wondered. Did he know I was in here?

His footsteps started up again. The doorknob jiggled, and I sucked in my stomach, holding my breath, my entire body pressing back against the wall, melting into it as best as I could. The door began pulling away from me slowly, panic continuing to rise inside me. This was it, I thought. He's found me. The door kept moving farther away. I was no longer hidden, but then Hunter stepped outside into the hall. I couldn't believe it. I thought I had been caught, but he was only closing the door.

He didn't shut it all the way. He left it open a crack. Then the sound of his footsteps faded down the hall.

I opened my mouth, gasping for air, my heart beating like a drum in my chest.

I had suspected that Hunter might be able to see, and now I knew he could. He was a serial killer, pretending to be blind.

Noises sounded from the kitchen: water flowing from the faucet, cupboard doors closing, plates clattering, footsteps shuffling across the tiled floor. I remained in the laundry room, listening and waiting for my chance to make a run for the door. I felt claustrophobic from being shut inside here. Just be patient, I told myself. Remain calm. But I didn't know how much longer I could tolerate staying here. The walls felt like they were closing in on me. The air was too thick to breathe.

I just hoped that Hunter thought I had left the house while he was on the phone and that he didn't suspect I was still here. But the longer he remained in the kitchen, the more I feared that he knew he had me trapped. Maybe he was intentionally staying in the kitchen to block my path so I couldn't leave. Was he waiting for me to grow impatient, make a mistake, and reveal my hiding spot?

I knew Eli would show up at my house soon, and I wouldn't be there. Would he suspect something was wrong?

My legs eventually grew tired, so I sat on the floor right behind the door. I continued to listen for Hunter and hoped I would hear Eli come to the door looking for me. Darkness thickened in the laundry room and in the hallway as the sun started to set. Its light no longer shone bright through the windows at the back of the house. Soon the only source of light came from the kitchen. It softly trickled through the crack in the laundry room door.

The clattering on the other side of the door continued. Eventually the smell of garlic filled the air. I knew there was no chance I could run past Hunter without getting caught. He needed to leave the kitchen.

A clicking sound pricked my ears, then Max's nose bumped against the laundry room door. I quickly stuck my foot out to stop it from opening. Max continued to sniff. *Please don't bark*, I thought to myself. *Please go away.*

The noises in the kitchen began to fade and Max disappeared. I sat there on the hard floor, wondering when I should make a run for it. Should I wait until Hunter goes to sleep? Or maybe I'll hear the back door close if he goes out for a walk.

I still wasn't sure whether he knew I was in here. If he did, he wouldn't be going anywhere. But why wasn't he coming after me? What was he planning on doing? The possibilities were beyond frightening. I couldn't allow myself to dwell on worst-case scenarios. That wasn't helping me at all. I had to focus on getting out of here.

Time wasn't my enemy, I told myself. It was important to be patient. I needed to wait for the back door to close. If that didn't happen, then I needed to wait even longer. If I ended up spending the entire night here, that would be okay, I tried to convince myself. Once morning arrived, then all I would have to do was wait for Nevin to show up. He wouldn't let Hunter hurt me. He had already protected me from Matt.

More time continued to pass. The house remained silent, and any hope I had for Eli to show up had pretty much vanished. He should have come over here by now. If he was truly worried about me, he would have exhausted all possibilities.

Hope was dwindling inside me. I knew the real worst-case scenario was that I wouldn't make it out of here alive. I worried about Mom and how she would handle the news of my death. I was glad that I hugged her before she left and that I had a chance to say goodbye. At least she had Tim to comfort her, and she wouldn't be alone.

I suddenly realized that I hadn't heard Max's claws clicking around on the floors lately, nor had I heard Hunter's footsteps.

I leaned close to the door, slowed my breathing, listening more carefully. There was something making a noise. It was subtle and faint. The sound carried through the air just barely. Was that Hunter breathing? Was he just outside the door? My stomach dipped, heart kicked around in my chest. I sat there motionless, all my muscles taut, wishing that I was already standing. That would make it easier to fight back and defend myself. But if I moved now, I might make too much noise. He would know where I was hiding.

CHAPTER 27

MILTON

Sharks have more than one method of attacking their victims. They might use a bump-and-bite technique, where they first circle their prey, then swim by and bump it, followed by going in for the bite.

Another type of attack is the sneak attack. Obviously with this one, there's no warning bump. It's just a lunge and bite. You won't see it coming. Then there's the swim right up and charge attack. With this one, you just might see it coming, but it will happen so quickly, you won't be able to get away.

How do you protect yourself from a shark? If you're in deep water and a shark is nearby, I would recommend never turning your back on it. You should always keep it in sight. How else will you be able to defend yourself? You need to be able to see it coming.

Sometimes people foolishly think if they remain quiet and

stop moving, that the shark will just swim away and leave them alone. A strategy like that would only work if the shark was blind. But I can see perfectly clearly. So that won't work with me.

CHAPTER 28

WINTER

I listened intently, wondering if my ears had deceived me. Was this the sound of Hunter breathing just outside the door, or was this the sound of him snoring from somewhere else in the house?

If Hunter was asleep, then this was my chance to escape. The closest exit was the back door. All I would have to do was pass through the kitchen, the family room, the back patio, and then I would be at the door.

I exhaled, shifting my body weight, and slowly stood up. My heart pounded as I carefully pulled the door open and stepped out into the hallway. Before entering the kitchen, I peeked around the corner, then froze. There was a light coming from the computer monitor in the family room. I could see Hunter sitting there in front of it. Luckily his back was facing me, otherwise he would have seen me. I considered hiding in the laundry room again, but I couldn't endure it—I had to get out of here.

From where I was standing, I was closer to the back door than Hunter was. The computer was located on the far side of the family room, the exact opposite side of the house as the back door. If I was quiet and careful, I might be able to slip behind Hunter unnoticed. If by chance he were to see me, I might still be able to escape if I was quick enough.

I stood there for another moment, trying to build up my courage. This might be my only chance, I told myself. Do it now. I took my first step into the kitchen, my eyes focused on Hunter. He was typing something on the keyboard. I could hear the faint clicking of the keys.

My vision continued to come into focus, adjusting to the light, and I realized that Max was lying next to Hunter's feet. I was halfway through the kitchen when I heard Max whine. I froze in place, holding my breath. Hunter turned his head. I saw the outline of his baseball cap, but the family room was too dark for me to see if he was looking at me. Then his arm moved, and I almost took a step back. No, I told myself. You're not going back there. You're getting out of here.

Hunter reached down, and I saw Max's silhouette. He placed something in Max's mouth then turned back to face the monitor again. I exhaled, my entire body shaking.

My best chance of getting out of here was now, while Max was still chewing on his dog treat. I moved carefully and swiftly, passing through the kitchen and into the family room. I watched Max and Hunter, my heart rate beating so fast, I felt like my chest would explode.

Slowly and quietly, I entered the enclosed patio. The moonlight trickled through the windows. I walked past the wicker sofa, then I heard that same noise again, and my heart leaped in my chest. I almost gasped audibly at what I saw. It was Hunter! He wasn't moving. He was lying there asleep.

CHAPTER 29

WINTER

If Hunter was in here sleeping on the couch, then the person at the computer must have been Nevin. Maybe Hunter isn't the killer, I thought. Maybe it's Nevin. He had access to Hunter's house. That glove and the blood-soaked towels might have been his. Hunter would never know it was there. This explanation made the most sense. Nevin wouldn't be able to keep those things in his apartment, because he lived with Eli.

I grabbed hold of the doorknob, turning it slowly, and eased the door open. The hot, humid air enveloped me as I slipped out into the dark night. I closed the door gently behind me. Then turned and ran.

I remembered that I had gone out the front door earlier. It should still be unlocked. When I ran around the corner to the front yard, I was surprised to see Jaxson standing on my front porch.

He pointed at me, eyes wide. "We've been looking all over for you. Where have you been?"

I glanced around but didn't see Eli. Was he inside my house? "Where is Eli?"

"He's around here somewhere. We've been trying to find you. We've been all over the neighborhood. He's totally freaking out. Why didn't you tell him you wouldn't be home?"

I didn't want to explain things to Jaxson right now. "Call him on your phone. Put it on speaker. I need to talk to him. It's urgent."

"Winter!" a deep voice called. I turned around and saw someone running toward us. They were several houses away. It was too dark for me to be sure, but it looked like it might be Eli.

"I'm here!" I shouted back, waving my arms.

"Winter!" he called again, and this time I knew it was Eli's voice.

"See, I told you he was looking for you," Jaxson said. "Where have you been? You can't just disappear like that. Eli was worried that you might end up dead in the ocean somewhere like those other girls."

Believe me, I was worried about that too, I wanted to say. But just then, someone stepped out onto Hunter's front porch. When I saw the hat, I knew it was Nevin.

I pointed at him as he started walking across the street. "Jaxson, go get him! Stop him!"

"What?"

"Go stop him! Hurry, he's getting away!"

Jaxson started running toward Nevin, and I followed at full sprint. I kept shouting for Nevin to stop, but he wouldn't. He picked up his pace.

Nevin had made it to the neighbor's fence and was about to climb over when out of the corner of my eye, Eli appeared. He grabbed Nevin by the shoulders and yanked him down to the ground.

"Get away from me!"

My eyes widened when I heard the voice, and then I saw the person's face. It wasn't Nevin. It was Tamara! Her hair had been pulled up and she was wearing a baseball cap.

"What were you doing in Hunter's house?" I asked.

Jaxson approached her, getting in her face. "Answer the question!" he yelled.

"I was just visiting. What did you think I was doing?"

"Stop lying!" I snapped. "I saw her in Hunter's house when Hunter was asleep. She was feeding Max treats to keep him quiet."

Jaxson grabbed her by the arm. "What were you doing in his house?" he demanded again.

Eli shined his phone at something in the grass, then bent down to pick it up. "Four credit cards," he said, shuffling through them. "These all belong to Hunter."

Jaxson leaned in close to her face. "You were stealing from a blind person?" his voice boomed, echoing in the air.

"She was using Hunter's computer," I said, "probably stealing money from his bank account too."

"Let's take her to your house and call the cops," Eli said. "Tell me what happened. Were you at Hunter's house this entire time?"

I started explaining what had happened. I described the glove with the blades that looked like shark teeth and the blood on the towels.

Jaxson dragged Tamara over to the couch in the living room. Then he turned to me, a confused expression on his face. "So you're saying that Hunter killed those girls and that he isn't really blind?"

Eli shook his head. I could sense the anguish and pain he was feeling. The look of devastation on his face made it clear. "Hunter is blind. He couldn't have killed those girls." He paused, looking down at the floor. "It had to have been Nevin."

Jaxson nodded his head slowly, his eyes wide with surprise. I had never seen him speechless before.

I held my hand out. "I need to borrow someone's phone so I can call the cops."

Jaxson grabbed his phone out of his pocket. "I'll call," he said. His eyes flicked over to Eli, who was standing there looking pale like he was gonna pass out. Jaxson stepped out onto the porch with the phone to his ear, leaving the door open.

I placed my hand on Eli's arm. "I'm sorry," I said, wishing he didn't have to go through this.

"Can't you guys just let me go?" Tamara asked. "You've got the credit cards. I didn't steal anything else."

I moved in front of her so that she would look directly at me. "You lied about knowing my aunt. Eli saw you with her. Why did you lie? Is it because you murdered her?"

Tamara pointed to the stairs. "Your aunt fell down those stairs. Why can't you just accept that? I may be a thief, but I'm not a murderer."

Liar! "Did you steal her engagement ring?"

She raised her eyebrows as if she was offended. "No. I stole from Hunter. You saw the credit cards. I tried to hack into his bank account on his computer, but I couldn't get through," she huffed. Then she turned to look at Eli. "I need to use the bathroom."

"You're not going anywhere," he replied.

"Sit on the floor," I demanded. "I don't want you peeing on my couch."

Tamara didn't move until Eli took a step toward her, then she slid off the couch and sat on the floor like I had asked her to. She got this weird look on her face and sort of smiled. "Nevin didn't kill those girls. If you let me go, I'll tell you who did."

"Nobody's letting you go," I snapped. "You are delusional."

She raised her shoulders. "Fine. Then I'll just keep it to myself."

"How do we know that you're not bluffing?" Eli asked. "How do we know you've got any real information to share?"

What was he doing? Tamara couldn't be trusted. There was

no way we should even consider listening to her ridiculous proposal.

Tamara pulled her knees into her chest. "You're going to have to trust me. I swear I know who it is. And it isn't your brother."

"She's lying," I said. "She doesn't know anything."

"You need to give us more information than that," Eli said, and I was starting to get nervous. Was he actually considering letting her go?

Tamara kept her attention focused solely on Eli. "You don't really want your brother to be falsely accused, do you?"

Jaxson came back inside the house. "Cops are on their way," he said.

I motioned for Eli to come with me out onto the porch. "Can I talk to you in private?" I looked over at Jaxson. "Watch her. Do not let her out of your sight."

A devious grin emerged on his face. He laced his fingers together and cracked his knuckles. "Oh, believe me. She isn't going anywhere."

Eli stepped out onto the porch with me. "What's wrong?"

"You can't really be considering letting her go, are you?" I glanced back through the doorway at her. "She's lying. That's all she ever does. She's a sociopath and can't be trusted."

He leaned in closer to my ear. "Don't worry about what I say to her. I'm just trying to get her to tell me what's going on. I promise you. I'm not going to make any deals. If Nevin didn't kill those girls and the real murderer isn't found, then more innocent people will die."

Flashing blue lights suddenly appeared in the distance. Both Eli and I turned to look. "That was fast," I said.

Jaxson cried out and my stomach dipped. We ran back into the house to see what was wrong. Jaxson was buckled over, holding his crotch, groaning in pain. And Tamara was gone.

"Where is she?" I gasped.

Jaxson dropped down to his knees, tears in his eyes. His words weren't coming across clearly, but he was looking toward the back of the house.

Eli and I took off running down the hallway. The sliding glass door had been left wide open. We both ran outside, heading straight for the beach. The moon was out tonight, which helped provide some light, but it was still hard to see.

"Let's split up," Eli said. "I'll go this way." He pointed over his shoulder.

I nodded in agreement. "Okay. I'll head the other way."

I ran as fast as I could, but my feet were sinking into the sand. Before long, I was gasping for air, struggling to keep going. Running after Tamara felt useless. She already had a head start. There was no way I could catch up to her. I wasn't fast enough. I didn't have the endurance. My only hope was that Eli had already found her. Or maybe the cops did. I turned back around, feeling too exhausted to continue.

By the time I made it back to the house, Eli was already standing in the backyard with a couple police officers.

"Did you find her?" I asked, my breath still labored, my

energy drained. Before he could even speak, the look on his face answered my question. I knew she was gone.

"No, I couldn't find her," Eli replied, sounding just as defeated as I felt. "I'm sorry."

"It's not your fault." I wanted to cry, but that would only make him feel worse. I had to keep it together. This wasn't his fault. I was the one who asked him to step out on the porch so we could talk. I should have trusted that he knew what he was doing. He wasn't going to give in to Tamara. He was only hoping he could clear his brother's name. He loved his brother, and I couldn't blame him for wanting to help.

The cops stepped aside to talk among themselves. I could hear radio chatter and other voices coming from inside the house.

I looked up into Eli's eyes, and I knew something else was wrong. "What is it?"

He narrowed his eyes. "Jaxson's gone."

"Isn't he out looking for Tamara?"

Eli's lips pressed together. He took a deep breath and shook his head. "The neighbor saw him drive away in his car with Tamara. She said that neither Tamara or Jaxson looked like they were being forced against their will." Eli raked his fingers through his curls as he looked at the open sliding glass door. "I think the back door was left open to draw us outside so that they could escape. Jaxson was faking being hurt."

My stomach knotted up. "So Tamara must have been hiding in the house."

"Yeah, I think that's what happened." Eli stared down at the ground, his hands in the pockets of his shorts.

"Then Tamara wasn't lying when she said that Nevin didn't kill those girls. She knew who the real killer was. It was Jaxson. That has to be why he helped her get away. He wanted to escape too."

Eli nodded in agreement.

I searched through my memories, wondering if there were signs or clues that I had overlooked. I thought about the day that Jaxson came into my house and got mad at Tamara. His behavior was way over the top. He had demonstrated how easily he could lose his temper over something so small as being rejected by a girl.

Then I remembered the first day I saw Jaxson on the beach and how he didn't act shaken or troubled even though he and Eli had just recently pulled a dead body out of the ocean.

Jaxson had been interviewed by a news reporter when the second victim's body was found. He had helped pull that body from the ocean too.

When I talked to Jaxson and Eli about the first victim, Jaxson eagerly described the condition of her body like it didn't bother him, and he probably would have continued to say more if Eli hadn't cut him off. This again demonstrated his lack of compassion or concern about the girl.

I looked over at Hunter's house as a police officer walked out the back door. Then I turned to Eli. "Did they find the glove and the towels in Hunter's house?"

"Yeah. They did. That stuff was still in the laundry basket like you said."

I didn't know why Jaxson had left his glove and the bloody towels at Hunter's house. Maybe he did it hoping that Hunter wouldn't see those things, yet he still should have been concerned about Nevin finding them. Whatever his reason for doing it, I was just grateful that I had found those things. The cops could figure out the rest.

Sirens sounded in the distance, and I couldn't help but wonder if Jaxson and Tamara had been caught. They couldn't have gone far, not yet anyway.

Eli's attention was on the activity next door at Hunter's, as more cops exited his house to search around his backyard.

I couldn't imagine what Eli was feeling. He was probably relieved that his brother wasn't the killer but at the same time, he had to have been devastated. He was probably searching through his memories too, trying to figure out if he had missed any signs or clues that Jaxson, his friend and coworker, didn't actually save lives. He took them.

CHAPTER 30

WINTER

Two days had passed since Tamara and Jaxson disappeared. They were still missing and on the run. The evidence seized from Hunter's house was being processed by the police.

The cops believed that Tamara was using an alias, which meant that it was going to make tracking her down a lot more complicated. Whether the cops would be able to prove that she murdered Aunt Emma and stole from her was yet to be determined.

I wondered if Jaxson and Tamara would be able to coexist, or if their personalities would clash too much. Maybe they had already separated and set off on their own. Or maybe they turned on each other. If that was the case, then who would be the victor, I wondered. They were both dangerous and evil. Jaxson had murdered three girls. Tamara had murdered Aunt

Emma and probably others as well. Jaxson was stronger, but Tamara seemed much smarter. This matchup would be a true test of brain versus brawn.

As I sat on the beach next to Eli, I couldn't help but wonder if the next wave that crashed would bring Tamara's dead body along with it.

The breeze in the air was light, the sun about to set. It was a miracle that Eli and I had this moment to ourselves. News reporters had been hounding us nonstop.

As we sat there soaking up the day's last rays of sunshine, I saw a woman walk by with a baby in her arms and my thoughts turned to Kyle. I hadn't finished telling Eli what happened to him. So I told him about the blanket I had made that caused Kyle to suffocate. "I feel like Kyle's death was my fault," I said.

Eli's eyes crinkled in the corners. "Wasn't your mom the one who decided to lay the blanket down over the mattress?"

"Well, yeah, but if I hadn't made that blanket, then Kyle wouldn't have died."

"And wasn't your aunt the one who laid Kyle down on his stomach to go to sleep that night?"

"Yes, but he still would have survived, if it hadn't been for that stupid blanket I made."

Eli repositioned his chair, moving it closer so that he could face me. He took a deep breath. "You know, Winter, I never did explain to you why Hunter hates me. It's not just because of the lies that Nevin told him."

Eli's head dropped below his shoulders as he gathered his thoughts. When he looked up at me again, there was a pained expression on his face. "Nevin and I were there the day that Hunter lost his eyesight. The three of us were upstairs throwing a football around, playing a game of keep-away. But the version of the game we played involved tackling each other. Hunter threw the ball to Nevin, and I ran to get it from him, but Nevin threw it back to Hunter before I could get there. I spun around and went after Hunter, trying to grab the football away from him. Hunter wasn't quick enough, so I tackled him, knocking him backward, right against the railing. It snapped like a twig, and he fell from the second story, down to the tiled floor below."

Eli's eyes glossed over and he took another deep breath. "Hunter never told his parents the part that I played in his accident. I think because Nevin begged him not to. So his parents sued Tim, since it was his employee who installed the railing incorrectly. When I went to visit Hunter in the hospital, he told me it was my fault that he couldn't see. He said I tackled him so hard that I caused the railing to break. He believed that it wasn't the construction worker's fault. But our combined body weight shouldn't have caused the railing to fail. It should have been sturdy enough to withstand the pressure." Eli paused a beat. "Anyway. That's why Hunter hates me. He still hasn't forgiven me. And even though I know the railing shouldn't have snapped, I feel responsible for what happened to Hunter."

"But it was an accident," I said. "You shouldn't feel guilty. It wasn't your fault."

Eli turned to look out at the ocean. I wondered if I should say something else, or if it was best for me to just stay quiet. Maybe I could talk to Hunter and help smooth things over. Maybe that would help Eli get over his guilt.

Eli took hold of my hand. He looked deep into my eyes. "Winter. You've told me that what happened to Hunter wasn't my fault. Now I'm going to tell you something that I want you to listen to very carefully... I have forgiven myself for what happened to Hunter. Are the memories still painful? Sure. Most definitely. Will I ever forget them? No, probably not. But I'm at peace. The stuff that happened with Kyle and Venus and her little brother and sister, I can tell that you're holding on to a lot of pain and guilt. But I want you to realize that no amount of personal anguish you put yourself through will ever make up for what happened. You can't change the past and neither can I, but you can move forward. What you need to do is to forgive yourself."

Tears came gushing out of my eyes, and I couldn't stop them. Eli held me in his arms while I cried.

Why was it so hard to forgive myself? Maybe because when you lose someone close to you, you're left with a hole inside your heart. An emptiness. All you have left are the memories and regrets. Maybe that hole inside of me could start to heal, if I focused on the good memories instead of the bad. Maybe it was possible to forgive myself.

I wondered if it was just by chance that Eli and I had met. Or if we were destined to be together. At that moment, right there on the beach, as he held me in his arms under the pink and purple sky, I began to feel something that I hadn't felt in a long time.

Hope.

I had been afraid to let anyone get close to me, because I didn't think I was worthy of their love. But despite what I had done in my past and the tragedies that had occurred, I was starting to believe that maybe I could move on and heal.

Those things that I had done didn't seem to have an effect on Eli. He, in his own way, had experienced tragedy, emotional pain, and guilt too, and he had overcome it. He wanted me to experience that same peace that comes from hope.

Hope was the opposite of fear. Fear pushed people apart, while hope pulled them closer together.

CHAPTER 31

TAMARA (BELLANY)

The night that Jaxson and I slipped away and escaped, I honestly didn't expect it to work. I thought for sure I was going to jail for the rest of my life. But then Eli and Winter made a huge mistake. They left me alone with Jaxson.

His eyes were wild, feet fidgeting. Beads of sweat rolled down his neck. I motioned for him to come over to me. I went all in on a gamble, with zero proof, only suspicion.

"You know…" I said, my voice low, "the cops are going to test for DNA. It won't be long before they find a match."

Jaxson's throat visibly tightened. He swallowed hard as his eyes darted around the room, and I knew… Hunter wasn't the killer. Jaxson was.

"My advice…" I whispered. "You should run before the cops get here."

"But—I didn't..." he stammered, wiping the sweat off his forehead.

I kept my gaze locked on to his. "I can help you escape," I said, my voice calm and reassuring. "I know exactly what to do."

Suddenly, anger flashed across his face. "Shut up," he snapped. "You don't know nothin'."

"I know you're about to get caught," I said. "But it doesn't have to end that way. I've got money. I've got enough for both of us to get out of here." I reached into my pocket and pulled out the enormous diamond ring. "This is worth at least a hundred thousand dollars, and I've already got a cash buyer lined up."

Jaxson's eyes nervously bounced between me, the ring, and the door. Winter and Eli were out on the front porch having their own private conversation, which I knew could end at any moment. There was no more time to waste.

"Please, Jaxson," I said, forcing tears into my eyes. "I'm begging you to save us—both of us."

Instantly, something seemed to switch on inside that head of his. There was a hunger in his eyes. Maybe it was the "begging you" comment that triggered it—I wasn't sure. All I knew was that Jaxson was down for whatever I was offering. He didn't ask any more questions. He didn't interrupt. He just listened intently, breathing heavily as more sweat poured down his face.

"I'll meet you at your car, okay?" I said.

"Yeah." He nodded.

Just as I turned to head to the back door, he grabbed hold of my arm, squeezing tight. "You better not be messing with me," he hissed into my ear, squeezing me even harder.

"I'm not messing with you," I assured him. "I need your help and you need mine."

Jaxson hesitated again. "Give me the ring."

"Jaxson, we can split the money, but—"

"Give it to me now, or the deal is off," he snarled.

I pulled the ring from my pocket, and he snatched it out of my hand.

It wasn't easy giving up control, but my plan was still in motion. This was just another wrinkle I would have to work out. Besides, he didn't know about the additional twenty grand in cash that I had stolen from Hunter. I had been siphoning money from Hunter's bank accounts for weeks.

When Jaxson and I took off in his car, I kind of expected him to set his doubts aside and put some trust in me, out of necessity if nothing else. But that entire night and continuing on into the next day, he gave off a twitchy, cornered-animal energy, constantly watching me. It was like he thought I would vanish the second he blinked, which was a fair assessment. I did plan on leaving him behind, but not yet.

"We just need to lay low for a few days," I told him, kicking my feet up on the motel nightstand. "Trust me, I've done this before. Three times, actually."

"You say that like it's supposed to be reassuring."

"Would you prefer a first-timer with clean hands and no clue what she's doing?"

His jaw tensed. "You know what I'd prefer? Just once in my life I'd prefer someone who didn't lie."

He was not living in reality. Everybody lies. "I know what you mean. I wanted the same thing from my boyfriend, Quentin, but look where that got me." I continued spinning the story of how I had been forced to go on the run, painting myself as the victim.

Suspicion oozed from Jaxson's squinted expression. "How about you cut the crap and tell me what really happened with Quentin?"

I let out a soft sigh, just enough breathiness to sound tragic. "Quentin used me. He manipulated me." I let my eyes get a little glossy. "He wasn't who I thought he was."

Jaxson's expression remained cold.

"I'm lucky to be alive," I added.

He jerked forward in his chair, fists clenched. "Your boyfriend ended up dead, and somehow you walked away with all the money. I doubt that was luck."

"You think I had something to do with his murder?" I asked, offended. "I loved Quentin."

He let out a bitter laugh. "Girls like you don't love. You attach yourself like a parasite, and then you destroy." Jaxson's face was hard as stone.

I couldn't take it anymore. "Are you done projecting?" I said, raising my voice. "Because if we are going to survive this together, you are going to have to stop assuming I'm just like one of your ex-girlfriends and start seeing me for who I really am."

Jaxson didn't respond. The silence stretched on for a while, and I just let it. I knew he kept the ring in the same pocket as that stupid shark tooth. I had to get it back somehow. A new strategy began to take shape.

I needed to calm Jaxson's fears and help him learn to trust me. I made it my mission to stroke his ego, telling him all the things he wanted to hear.

I complimented him, asked for his advice, hung on his every word, did all I could to help boost his confidence. I intentionally acted like I was the weaker person. I would say things to him like, *I can't get this remote control to work. Can you help me? I can't unscrew this jar of peanut butter. Could you do it for me? I can't figure out which hotel to stay at. Should we choose one in town or should we stay somewhere less crowded?*

These little insignificant things began adding up, and finally Jaxson was starting to relax around me. That was when I told him a made-up childhood sob story, claiming that I had been abandoned by my parents and how it traumatized me.

I cried on his shoulder, giving him a chance to comfort me. He pet my head, holding me in his arms, and said, "It's going to be okay. We have each other now. You don't have to worry about me abandoning you. I'll always be here for you."

If he could have seen my face right then, I would have blown everything. He would have known I was lying. I wanted to laugh at the absurdity of it all, and at the same time I wanted to celebrate, because I had done it. I had slowly chipped away at his defenses. He was finally starting to trust me.

I never told Jaxson about my past names, Bellany and Charity. I lied to him about where I had lived, what I had done, and why I had been on the run from the cops. He didn't need to know that information. I wanted him to believe that I was not a threat to him and that we both had the same goal—to avoid getting caught by the police.

Jaxson told me all about his past, how he had gone by the name Milton Thorne and pretended to be blind. He explained, in detail, how he had murdered his victims; how he had no choice. As far as he was concerned, those girls made him do it. "I never would have killed them, if they had just shown me some respect." He squeezed my hand a little too hard, eyes boring through me, trying to intimidate me. But I have never been the type to get intimidated—I get even.

I pretended like I didn't feel any pain or discomfort from his tight grip. The look on my face was full of compassion. "They should have treated you better. I mean, what kind of person takes advantage of someone who's blind?" I recognized the pure irony coming from my lips. *I* was just like those girls. I had stolen from Hunter and he was actually blind. But Jaxson didn't catch it.

Sometime after midnight we stopped at a motel. We were both tired from driving all day. I took the bed closest to the bathroom and made him take the one by the door. I really wanted to try and get some sleep, but I had figured out that when Jaxson got tired he tended to be less guarded.

When I felt like it was safe to bring up, I asked him why he left all that incriminating evidence in Hunter's house.

"That wasn't my original plan. The cops were patrolling the street. I had to stash it somewhere, and I thought it would be safe in Hunter's house. I knew he wasn't home, because I had already seen him out on the beach with his annoying dog."

Hiding a bloody glove and towels in Hunter's house was a big risk. Sure, he might be able to fool a blind guy, but what about Nevin? "When were you planning on going back to get it?" I asked, climbing under the covers.

Jaxson flopped back onto a pillow, staring up at the ceiling. "I didn't forget, if that's what you're implying. I was gonna take care of it, but then Eli begged me to help him look for Winter. I knew Eli was going to be wandering around and might see me sneaking into Hunter's house, so I had to wait." Jaxson rolled onto his side to look at me, a scowl on his face. "Everything would have worked out fine if that albino hadn't decided to play detective."

"Yeah, totally," I nodded like I agreed with him. But it didn't surprise me at all that Winter had stumbled into his secrets. What amazed me was that his killing spree had gone on as long as it had. He was careless and foolish, using an unsustainable disguise to hunt in the same tiny pool over and over again. "So how did you get into his house anyway? Did you have a key?"

"He keeps a spare under the mat, like an idiot."

I never searched for a spare key. Once I saw Max's doggy door, I knew I had a way in. Max never barked at me, because I always brought him treats.

I closed my eyes, about to fall asleep, but then Jaxson started talking again. He told me about his childhood, about all of the abuse, the trauma, the entire annoying story. He kept me up all night. Every time I was about to doze off, I tried to wake myself up by saying something thoughtful and supportive like, *That must have been so hard. How could they treat you that way? I'm so sorry you had to go through that.*

Despite being overly tired, I committed everything he said to memory. Information like that can sometimes prove to be helpful.

The next morning, he unexpectedly kissed me with his stinky breath. I wanted to vomit in his throat, but I kept my composure. I would be rid of him soon enough.

Before another long day on the road, we had to stop to get gas. I went inside the convenience store and found a little crystal shark figurine on display at the register. A few miles down the road I pulled it out and gave it to Jaxson. His eyes got all misty. I swear the idiot was about to cry.

"I think you're my soulmate," he sniffed.

I blushed, playing along. "I think you're mine too."

Then he leaned over and kissed me again. Luckily I had bought some breath mints while I was in the store to keep me from puking.

After another long day of traveling, we stopped at a hotel for the night. I was in bed, about to fall asleep when I felt Jaxson slide in behind me. I jumped up, flicking the lights on.

"What?" Jaxson hissed, glaring at me. "I can't sleep with you?"

I pointed to the other bed. "You're sleeping over there. By yourself."

"What about earlier today? You were like all into me. Or was that all an act? Are you trying to manipulate me or something? Is that what you're doing?"

I knew this would happen eventually. But the thought of being with him repulsed me. I could barely tolerate kissing him. It literally made me feel sick, because all I could think about was what he had done to those girls.

"I'm not trying to manipulate you, Jaxson. That's never been my intention."

"Oh really?" he said in his typical snarky tone. "Then what's the problem?"

"I'm saving myself for marriage."

His face scrunched up, eyes blinking. "What?"

I crossed my arms over my chest, eyes glossy. "I'm waiting for marriage."

"You mean you've never—"

"Never," I cut him off, pointing to his bed. "You're sleeping over there."

"Well, can't we at least kiss a little or something?" he countered, remaining right where he did not belong. In my bed.

"No. I'm tired. We stayed up all night last night talking. I need some sleep and so do you." If he kept fighting me on this, it was not going to end well for him. I was going to have to do something drastic.

Reluctantly, he finally peeled himself off my bed and flopped back onto the other one.

I laid down, unable to relax and fall asleep for the longest time. Normally Jaxson snored, but tonight, the room was eerily quiet.

Suddenly his bed squeaked. I heard him rip his covers off, and my muscles tensed. I couldn't see what he was doing. The room was pitch black, except for the glow of a tiny red light coming from the TV. I heard footsteps, then the groan of the bathroom door's hinges. Something inside me told me to get out of there. I rolled over and flung my covers off, but then I heard more movement. Again, the bathroom door squeaked. I laid in bed, perfectly still as if I were asleep.

Jaxson's footsteps shuffled slowly in my direction, then stopped. I could sense his presence beside my bed. He was so close now. Hovering. Watching me. His breath thick and heavy. I thought I had more time, but I was wrong. I should have killed him when I had the chance.

CHAPTER 32

TAMARA (BELLANY)

I laid in bed pretending to be asleep, while Jaxson continued to watch me. He stood next to my bed, hovering over me for what seemed like hours. The only thing I could think to do was remain completely frozen and not move an inch. Eventually, I heard him moving around. He dragged a chair across the floor and it sounded like he sat in it, but I didn't dare open my eyes to check.

As morning light slowly penetrated the darkness of our hotel room, I decided it was time to pretend like I was finally waking up. Jaxson had strategically placed his chair in front of the door. He had a wild look in his eyes again. "Are you okay?" I asked him, pretending to be oblivious to the fact that he hadn't slept at all last night.

"Did you have a good night's sleep?" he asked.

I nodded. "Yeah, I slept like a rock. What about you?"

"I couldn't sleep."

"Oh really?" I replied, acting surprised. "Well, maybe you'll be able to sleep better tonight." I smiled as if everything in the world was right. "We've got a big day ahead of us. I'm gonna start getting ready."

I stepped into the bathroom and locked the door. It was the first moment of relief I had felt in hours. When I came out, Jaxson was packed and ready, still planted in front of the door.

Once we left the hotel, he never let me out of his sight, except for when I went to use the restroom at Waffle House.

Our next stop of the day was the public library. We picked a corner table, set some books down in front of us, and waited. Jaxson still seemed on edge, but I acted oblivious. Jaxson pulled Emma's diamond ring out of his pocket and twirled it between his fingers. He nudged me, drawing my attention, and took hold of my hand.

"One day I'm gonna buy you another ring just like this one," he said. "I promise I will. And then I'm going to get down on one knee." He shifted off his chair, dropping a knee to the floor.

Huh. Look at that. He actually did it.

He looked up at me longingly, my hand in his, like we were starring in a low-budget rom-com. "And one day," he continued, "I'm going to ask you to marry me."

It took every ounce of self-control I had to act like I was in love with him. How could he even think I would want to marry him? He repulsed me. But I had to play along and pretend like

I was flattered. "Are you really going to propose to me someday? Do you really want to marry me?" I asked. But of course he did. I was thousands of miles out of his league. He could never, not in a million years, wind up with someone like me.

Jaxson slid the ring onto my finger. "Tamara, will you marry me?"

If I told him no, he would probably kill me. I gushed even more, pretending like I was the luckiest girl on the planet. "Yes, Jaxson. I *will* marry you."

We kissed and embraced, and I nearly lost my breakfast. I took a couple deep breaths. He held my hand in his, looking down at the ring as it sat perched on my finger. Then he looked back at me again, unaware of the real reason I was smiling.

"I know we need to sell this ring today," he said, "but I really wish we could keep it. My fiancée deserves to have an amazing ring."

I held my hand out, admiring the ring, thinking about everything I had done leading up to this moment.

If Jaxson knew the truth about my past and that I had murdered people too, I doubted he would still be interested in marrying me. My most recent kill was Emma. She was starting to suspect that I wasn't really Tamara Gold. I had caught her snooping around on my computer and my phone. The last thing I needed was for her to figure out that my real name is Bellany Silverfield, or to figure out that I had also used the name Charity Baker. There was no way I was going to let her ruin my life.

After Emma took her unfortunate tumble down the stairs, which I had caused, I called 911, pretending like I was her, gasping for help. Then I went out to the beach and soaked up the sun for the rest of the day, admiring her engagement ring. It fit perfectly on my finger.

She had originally buried it under the lifeguard tower like my letter instructed her to do. She was afraid for her life, and rightly so.

After she was gone, I was able to collect all the threatening letters I had written; all except for the one that was in her post office box. I almost had it in my hands when Winter caught me digging through her purse. I eventually did get my hands on it, though. I was spying on her when she slipped it into the book on the shelf.

I remember when Emma got that first letter. She was all frantic and scared. Her hands were trembling when she showed it to me. She wanted to call the police.

"Sure," I said, "call the police. And when your body washes up on the beach, I'll be sure to tell them how brave you were."

She blinked. "But what if they figure out who sent it?"

I gave her my best concerned-friend look. "The letter specifically said they'd kill you if you go to the police. Do you really want to risk your life over a ring?"

That shut her up. She was genuinely terrified. So I offered to help bury the ring. She didn't want to do it alone, and I was happy to assist.

I would have gotten rid of that letter myself—burned

it, shredded it, whatever—but I couldn't find the key to Emma's post office box. I looked everywhere, tossing out her personal junk as I searched for it, room by room. Still nothing.

After the new owners moved in, I couldn't believe my luck. Sasha and Winter offered me an ideal situation. By living in the house with them, I got to kill two birds with one stone. I would be able to destroy the letter, while also having ready access to Hunter's house. Stealing from a blind person—it couldn't get much easier than that.

Jaxson slammed a library book down on the table, snapping me back to the present. "Do you think this guy's still coming or what?"

I patted his knee, smiling. "Be patient. Guys like this aren't always punctual, but it's not a big deal. He said he was coming. I know he'll show up with the money."

Jaxson opened up another book about sharks, grumbling to himself. As he flipped through the pages, he started lamenting over what had happened with Winter, how he hated Eli for stealing her away from him.

I wanted to take that book and hit him over the head with it. He had just proposed to me, and now he had the audacity to bring up another girl? Of course I didn't really want to marry him, but still. He had just insulted me.

"I know Winter would have been mine," he said as he flipped another page. "But then Eli had to swoop in and steal her away." He slammed his book shut, eyes flicked up to meet mine. "She deserved to die for rejecting me. She used me just to get to Eli."

Jaxson started going over all of the things that had gone wrong. He whined about how he had accidentally broken his night vision goggles and had to use a flashlight instead. "It would have been perfect. The power had gone out. I was going to show up at her house, knock on the door, and ask to hang out. I planned on leaving one of the windows cracked open for easy access later, but I never made it to the front door. Tim came running out of the house and chased me down the street, acting like he was gonna cut my head off," he said through gritted teeth. "I should have never shined my flashlight in the windows. All that did was freak them out." He slammed his fist down on the table. "It should have been Winter who died that night, not that random girl I found walking along the beach."

"Jaxson, calm down," I said, my voice low.

He snatched me by my wrist and squeezed. "Where is this guy?"

"Let go," I pleaded like I was helpless. "Please, Jaxson."

He shoved my arm away, still agitated. Then he jabbed his finger right in front of my face. "You better not be screwing with me. He better show up."

I held my wrist, acting like I was in more pain than I really was, tears rolling down my cheeks.

"Hey, I'm sorry," he said. "I didn't mean to hurt you."

Yes, you did. Jaxson's extreme mood swings and his angry

outbursts were unpredictable, and they were getting worse. I ran my finger under my eyes to wipe the tears away. "My makeup is smearing," I sniffed. "I need to go wash my face."

As I stood up to go to the restroom, he grabbed my arm. "You're staying with me."

"Jaxson, my face is a mess. I can't meet our buyer looking like this."

"I'm coming with you."

"You need to stay here and keep an eye out for him. If he shows up and we're not here—"

"Fine! You've got one minute. Hurry up."

I didn't go to the restroom. I had already arranged for a taxi to pick me up in front of the library. I jumped into the back seat and told the driver I would tip him a fifty if he'd drive like he was on the run from the police. His foot mashed down on the gas pedal, and we sped off out of the parking lot.

As I watched the world sail by through the side window, I thought about the night of the thunderstorm. Jaxson's plans weren't the only ones that got botched that night. I was going to kill Winter, smother her with her own pillow while she was asleep. I had overheard Sasha talking about Kyle. She was telling the entire story to Tim. Sasha mentioned that Winter had made the blanket that smothered Kyle. So I figured Winter should have the same fate as her dead brother.

Sasha also told Tim about what happened when Winter's friend was killed. She said that she wasn't sure if she believed Winter's story. She thought Winter knew in advance that

Chaz had brought a gun. If Winter was capable of setting up her friend like that, I knew she was capable of coming after me. So I had planned on killing her that night.

But my plans were ruined when the power went out. Sasha came to check on Winter, and I thought I had been caught. But foolishly, Winter didn't check under her bed, where I was hiding. As soon as they went upstairs, I slipped back downstairs and pretended like nothing had happened.

"Is this the right gas station?" the taxi driver asked.

"Yes. Pull in over by the dumpster. I will be right back."

The transaction happened quickly. I sold Emma's ring and walked away with a backpack full of cash. It was nothing close to the ring's actual value, but it was still a huge score.

"Where to now?" the driver asked.

I wasn't exactly sure yet. Maybe I would go to Florida, or maybe Georgia. I could go anywhere I wanted. I was free and that was all that mattered. What would my new name be? I kind of liked Athena. After all, I sure felt like a Greek goddess.

"Get on the freeway," I said, pointing to the sign.

I wondered what Jaxson was doing right now. What would his future hold? I figured he was either going to end up wandering around the streets begging for money and food, or he was going to end up behind bars. I would prefer it if he were behind bars, which was why I called the police and tipped them off to his location.

READ ON FOR A SNEAK PEEK AT THE NEXT IN THE SERIES

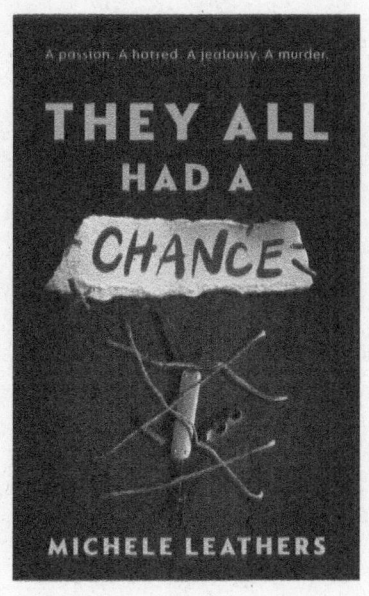

PROLOGUE

JANE

I never should have agreed to do this. I clamped my eyes shut as soon as those negative thoughts entered my mind. A drop of sweat slowly rolled down the side of my face. I pried my eyes open again. *Keep going, Jane,* I told myself, trying to overcome the paralyzing fear that had seized me.

I loosened my grip and once again began falling. The sensation from rappelling made my stomach flutter like I was riding on a rollercoaster. I slowly moved my right hand toward the small of my back, gripping the rope firmly. The figure eight attached to my harness did its job, stopping my descent. I leaned back, staring up at the entrance to the cavern, my heart pounding wildly. I wasn't afraid of falling. The panicked feeling growing inside me had nothing to do with that. What worried me was what I might find after the descent.

Thoughts of regret and an overwhelming sense of doom

continued to swirl inside my mind. I inhaled, drawing in a deep breath, but there didn't seem to be enough oxygen in the air. I fell deeper into despair, the further I descended into the cavern.

If only I hadn't come back here this summer, then I wouldn't be in this mess. But my aunt and uncle insisted, and I didn't have a choice. At first, my uncle tried to convince me by bringing up the subject of money.

"If you work at Camp Sunshine this summer, you'll be able to afford to do fun things while you're away at college with Carla. You two like getting your nails done and going shopping, right? You'll need some money to do things like that."

My aunt and uncle didn't know that Carla and I were no longer best friends. We had a huge fight a couple weeks earlier. She said she was never going to speak to me again. I didn't blame her for hating me. I had messed up – big time – but I was too ashamed to tell my aunt and uncle what had happened.

"I've got enough money saved up from working at camp last summer," I insisted, which was a lie. I hadn't counted my money lately. My best guess was that I only had about forty dollars left. But I didn't need any more money than that.

I planned on spending my summer doing things that didn't cost me any money, like binge watching shows on Netflix and Amazon, walking to the library to check out a couple books each week, and learning how to cook by watching tutorial videos on YouTube.

This was going to be my last summer before college. I wanted it to be lowkey and relaxing. My college tuition had already been paid for, including room and board. If I ended up needing more money after the semester started, I figured I could always get a job then. Bottom line, I didn't need to work at Camp Sunshine this summer.

My aunt's face contorted as she let out a heavy sigh. "Listen, Jane. Your uncle has been trying to be polite about this, but we both agree that it's time you start acting like an adult. You've graduated from high school, and you're almost eighteen."

"What do you mean, *act like an adult?*" I asked, confused. I had never been a rebellious or ungrateful teen. I never talked back to my aunt and uncle. I didn't understand what they wanted from me.

"Acting like an adult means that you provide for yourself," my uncle explained. "It means you stop relying on us and make your own way in the world. We've done our best to prepare you for this, and we think you're ready."

My aunt nodded in agreement. "If your mother had been given some tough love when she was your age, then maybe she would have turned out to be a responsible adult instead of a drug addicted homeless person."

I always hated it when she tried to throw that in my face. My mom was a screw up, and I was well aware of this, mostly because my aunt took every opportunity to remind me.

She continued to lecture me about how tough love was for my own good, before informing me that, as far as she was concerned, she had met her obligation and was no longer responsible for taking care of me.

She said, "It's time that you move out."

Move out? I couldn't believe it. I wasn't some unwanted houseguest who had overstayed their welcome. I had lived with them since I was seven. They adopted me. This was my home, and according to the law, they were legally responsible for taking care of me until I became an adult. My eighteenth birthday was still a month away. How could they do this to me? It was so unfair.

My uncle smiled at me like this was a happy occasion. He placed his hand on my shoulder, and I backed away, lengthening the distance between us.

"Don't act like that, Jane," My aunt scolded, like I was a disobedient child. If she and my uncle only knew how lucky they were. They had no idea how bad I could have been, or how much trouble I could've gotten into.

I didn't go out drinking and partying. I went to school like I was supposed to. I did my homework. I studied for tests, and I got good grades. I cleaned the house and helped with yard work. I did all of those things, because I wanted my aunt and uncle to treat me like I was their daughter. But they never fully accepted me. They never once told me that they were proud of me or that they loved me.

"I'm not even eighteen yet," I said in a dejected tone.

"Stop overreacting," my aunt snapped.

"It's not like you're going to be homeless," my uncle said.

"Catalina Island is a beautiful place. You're lucky to have an opportunity to go there and work at Camp Sunshine. You'll be provided with a place to live and food to eat, plus you'll be able to earn some extra money for college."

Tears stung my eyes. I knew I didn't have enough money to move out on my own, and Carla would never allow me to move in with her. I had no other choice but to return to Camp Sunshine, even though the thought of going back to that place absolutely horrified me.

I never told my aunt and uncle what happened at Camp Sunshine last summer. I hadn't told anyone. I thought I could just leave the past behind me, that it would somehow just vanish like it never happened. But I still had nightmares. I still thought about what happened all the time. And the police were still looking for Barkley Collins.

"Jane," a voice called from above, ripping me from my thoughts. As I squinted in the sunlight pouring through the opening of the cavern above me, I saw long blonde hair tumble forward. A hand quickly swept it back, revealing cold, menacing blue eyes. Why was she looking at me so strangely? She had insisted that I go first and seemed genuinely concerned about my wellbeing. But now I wasn't so sure. Something wasn't right.

"If I were you, I'd hurry up," she said in an ominous tone. Then a glint of light flashed, and when I saw what she was holding in her hand, my entire body jumped. Rocks and dirt broke free as I lost my footing. I hung there suspended in mid-air, staring death in the face, and her name was Athena.

ACKNOWLEDGMENTS

I want to thank my husband, Ryan, who lovingly tolerates my obsession with writing and all things Harry Potter—sometimes even humoring me by wearing the matching Hogwarts shirt I picked out for him. That's true magic.

A huge thank-you to Meg Gibbons for believing in this series, to Shannon Thompson for her insights and suggestions, and to all those behind the scenes at Sourcebooks without whom this would not be possible.

Thanks to Denise for her constant enthusiasm, cheerleading, and sympathetic ear.

To the readers, whether you have been with me from the start of my writing journey or have just joined, I'm grateful to you. Thank you for reading, for sharing, and for helping me to keep turning the page.

ABOUT THE AUTHOR

Michele Leathers's novels are fast-paced and full of jaw-dropping twists that will keep readers guessing till the end. She received a bachelor's degree in philosophy from North Carolina State University and is a full-time writer. She's not ashamed to admit that she's addicted to Diet Pepsi, chocolate, and writing. She's a shrewd observer of people, always looking for ideas and inspiration for her books.

sourcebooks fire

Home of the hottest trends in YA!

Visit us online and
sign up for our newsletter at
FIREreads.com

....

Follow
@sourcebooksfire
online